Rusty Peruke works as a mechanic and is close with his family. His wheelchair-bound brother, Korvyn, lives with him, and he sends extra cash home to his parents on a regular basis. When he meets Acheron while the man is at the shop buying a set of fast wheels, Rusty is both excited and concerned—and it's not because he's never been with a guy. Acheron is a loner scorpion shifter who hasn't stayed in one place since he left his family home over eight decades before. Rusty has no intention of running out on his family. To him, their needs come first. Can two polar opposites find enough common ground to build a future? Or will assumptions and miscommunications create a wall between them that's impossible to scale?

The Scorpion and His Prey
Copyright © 2018 Charlie Richards
ISBN: 978-1-4874-2075-8
Cover art by Angela Waters

Published by eXtasy Books Inc or
Devine Destinies, an imprint of eXtasy Books Inc
Look for us online at:
www.eXtasybooks.com or www.devinedestinies.com

The Scorpion and His Prey
Kontra's Menagerie: Book Twenty-Four

By

Charlie Richards

DEDICATION

Having someone to love is family. Having somewhere to go is home. Having both is a blessing.
~Unknown

CHAPTER ONE

"You about done there?"

Wiping the cloth over the side of the *Kawasaki* Ninja 250R, Rusty Peruke rose from where he crouched. He turned and focused on his boss, Jethro. Tucking the cloth into his belt, he nodded.

"Yeah," Rusty confirmed, taking a step back to admire the motorcycle he'd just finished wiping down. "It's a very pretty bike. Who's picking it up again?"

"One of Kontra's new pack members," Jethro told him, referencing a grizzly bear shifter who led a semi-nomadic biker gang. He shoved his hands into his pockets as he focused on the bike, too. "And, yep, this is definitely one fine machine. Uh, a guy named Acheron." Jethro chuckled a little as his blue eyes twinkled. "They would have swung by yesterday, but they were still finishing up his identity paperwork."

Rusty cocked his head, processing that. It clicked. "Oh, Acheron is one of the men Kontra's people rescued, and he turned out to be"—he took a quick glance around to confirm they were still alone in the display showroom floor—"a scorpion shifter."

Jethro nodded. "Yeah. That's the one."

"Damn. Glad they got those men out of there."

Rusty had heard the stories. A crow shifter had run across a bunch of young men locked in a small storage room of a warehouse. He'd flown toward town in search of help and had run across Kontra and his gang at a trailhead parking

1

lot. The group of shifters had rescued the kidnapped men, taking out most of the Diamondback biker gang in the process.

Unfortunately, the assholes who'd planned to buy the young men had come around. Jethro had told him that Kontra's people had lured the buyers out of town to deal with them. The repercussions were that the humans had learned of the paranormal world. At least a dirty deputy had been taken out, too.

Rusty was glad he didn't have to deal with that kind of crap. While some might think being a mechanic was boring, at least his steady, regular work allowed him to care for his brother, Korvyn, and send cash home to his parents. That was more than enough for him.

"Ah, this must be them."

Upon hearing Jethro's words, Rusty noticed the steadily increasing roar of a number of motorcycles. He peered out the window and spotted five motorcycles pulling into their lot... as well as one *Can-am* Spyder. Excitement flooded him as he saw the black and steel-gray three-wheeled vehicle being driven by Adam Kingston, a white tiger shifter.

"I didn't know Adam was bringing that today! Sweet!" Rusty strode swiftly toward the showroom's front door, grinning broadly. "Did you know?"

Jethro chuckled. "Surprise." He flanked him. "Yeah, I knew."

Rusty held the door open for his boss and friend, punching him in the shoulder as he passed, taking care to temper his shifter strength. Sharing his psyche with a serval cat, he was stronger and hardier than a human. It wasn't until recently that Rusty had been able to share that part of himself with Jethro, since shifters used anonymity and secrecy to keep themselves safe.

Just a few months before, Jethro had met a guy named

Wilhelm. The slightly heavyset, gray-haired male was a shifter who shared his life with a pygmy hippopotamus. Jethro had been brought into the paranormal world, as well as come out of the closet, and was now a very happy human in a relationship with a loving husband.

There were times Rusty felt a little jealous, but only because he'd love to find his mate, not because he had any attraction to either Jethro or Wilhelm.

Rusty watched Kontra and his people choose a place to settle their bikes. Once they began lowering their kickstands, he started toward them. He recognized their leader, Kontra, and the man behind him on the bike, his mate, Tim—who happened to be a warlock.

The others in the group were Payson, a hyena shifter, who had his human mate, Land with him. Noah, Adam's moose shifter mate, was driving Adam's *Harley*. The final pair of bikes were driven by the mated pair Lamar, a peacock shifter, and his human mate, Rueben. Both men had people Rusty didn't recognize behind them.

A slender, grinning, black-skinned man swung off the bike from behind Rueben. A slightly pale Caucasian sat behind Lamar. From the looks of things, the peacock shifter was reassuring the young man.

Stopping beside Adam, who was easing off the *Can-am*, Rusty spread his arms as he swept his gaze appreciatively over the machine. "Wow, Jethro didn't tell me you were bringing this today. It's gorgeous."

Adam shoved his hands into his pockets as he grinned broadly at him. His green eyes twinkled. "Got a call from a buddy in a town four hours away yesterday evening. Had to drive all night, but I couldn't wait to get my hands on this baby." The tiger shifter swiped his palm over the dark gray fender covering the front wheel nearest him in obvious admiration. "I got two days to spend with her before I need to

3

head home, so we'll see how much of the modification we can get done in that time."

Surprised by the offered help, Rusty gaped. "Wow, thanks, but aren't you supposed to be on vacation?"

"Oh, don't worry about that." Noah stopped next to his big lover, wrapping his arm around Adam's waist. "Working on this *is* a vacation to Adam."

Adam grinned as he turned his attention to Noah. He cradled the man's jaw and dipped his head, sealing his lips over them. When the kiss turned from a soft peck to something more carnal, Rusty returned his focus to the bike.

Jethro stopped next to him as they were joined by the others. "So, which one of those young men is Acheron?" he asked, glancing at the pair of short, slender males inspecting the bikes lined up along the sidewalk in front of the store.

Kontra chuckled. "The black guy there is your sure sale today, but I wouldn't call him a young man. He told me he's one hundred thirty-two." Winking, he added, "But don't worry. That's not what we put on his driver's license." Pointing at the blond man, Kontra added, "And that's Louis. Since his buddy Deter mated with Marrakesh, and they're going to be traveling with us, Louis decided he wants to join us. For now, I think he's just looking."

Nodding, Jethro headed their way. "Sounds good. Introduce me?"

Payson grinned widely, his gray eyes sparkling mischievously. "Yo, Acheron! Louis! Come over here a sec."

The blond spun, his blue eyes wide, clearly startled. Acheron wrapped one dark arm around his shoulders and guided him toward the group. Louis was clearly unsettled by the prospect of approaching so many big men, the acrid smell of his unease wafting on the breeze.

Rusty noticed another smell, too. It was earthy and masculine, yet still fresh, and reminded him of walking in a cool forest. It also caused his blood to heat and flow south. He swallowed hard as he glanced between the two men.

One of them is my mate!

When Acheron's black eyes widened and his nostrils flared, Rusty didn't need to be a genius to realize which one it was, either.

Acheron's full dark lips curved into a wide smile, and his eyelids slid to half-mast. "Oh, my," he murmured, his voice surprisingly deep for such a small man. Releasing his hold on Louis, the slender male stepped into Rusty's space. He rested his right hand on Rusty's chest and his left on his hip. Tipping his chin up, Acheron peered at him from beneath his lashes. "Hello, my pretty kitty."

Rusty sucked in a harsh breath as surprise filled him. Another burst of Acheron's heady scent filled his nostrils, too. Goose bumps broke out on his forearms, and his fingers twitched. Even his mouth watered for a taste of the shifter currently pressed against his side.

Lifting his hands, Rusty gave in to the urge to touch. He rested his hands on Acheron's hips. Then he slid his right one up his back, smoothing along his lean form.

Acheron hummed, his body undulating slightly as he rubbed against him. Peering at him with a hungry expression, he met Rusty's gaze fully. "Hmmm, are you shy?" he asked softly, sliding the fingertips of his right hand over Rusty's left nipple lightly. His smile turned hungry. "Cat got your tongue?"

His stomach clenching and sparks dancing across his skin, Rusty struggled to find his tongue. "H-Hi."

Gods, I sound like an idiot.

"Hi, yourself," Acheron murmured back, his voice husky. Teasing his fingertips over Rusty's name where it was stitched on his work shirt, then back to his nipple, he asked, "You work here? Is Rusty your real name?" He slid his left hand up Rusty's back, then scraped his nails back down again, caressing his spine. "Like fast bikes?"

"I do work here," Rusty confirmed. His voice sounded rough even to his own ears. He cleared his throat, then continued, "Yeah, my name's Rusty. I'm a mechanic." His mind was a bit sluggish, what with the petting stimulating his nerve endings. "No, fast bikes are a good way to get hurt. Can't help my family if I'm hurt."

"Helping family is admirable." Acheron cocked his head as he smiled up at him. "Knowing what to do with your cock is even more admirable." His expression turned hungry. "Do you?"

"What?"

Of course, Rusty had never considered himself an extremely eloquent man. He spoke to the machines he worked on more than people. Clearing his throat, he moved his left hand so he could grip Acheron's, stopping the teasing to his nipple that was causing his blood to fire in his veins. Rusty focused on the other shifter's dark eyes, seeing the merriment dancing within their depths.

"A mechanic means you're good with your hands, right?" Acheron waggled his brows as he growled softly. "Do you know what to do with this big shlong you're sporting for me, too?"

Unease slithered through Rusty.

"You are making fun of me," Rusty mumbled, frowning at Acheron. He moved his hands to Acheron's upper arms and took a step backward, separating them. "We are mates." Rusty paused just long enough to glance around and make certain there were still no others but his boss and Kontra's people. "And the first thing you do is... give me shit about whether or not I can use my dick?"

Acheron's eyes widened, and his lips parted. It was his mate's turn to feel shocked. When Acheron opened his mouth wider, probably to say something, Rusty lifted his hand, stalling him. He wasn't certain he wanted to hear an excuse, especially as another thought hit him.

"You're the one here for the *Kawasaki*. That's why you asked about fast bikes." Knowing it was a fact, that's how Rusty said the comment. "And I might be a shifter, but I do like to take my time." He lifted his hands and took another step backward. "How about I get your number off your purchase paperwork, and I'll call you? We can set up a date. Go to dinner." When his cat grumbled in his mind at the idea of getting a little space from his mate, Rusty mentally shushed the creature. "We'll get to know each other." Turning to Adam, he held out his hand. "Can I get the keys, Adam? Or would you like to drive it around back?"

While Adam's brows were furrowed, he slowly nodded. "I'll drive it around back." Noah glanced between them, but didn't comment when his mate cupped his jaw, pecked a kiss to his lips, and told him, "I'll be back out in a bit, babe."

Rubbing the back of his neck, Rusty forced a tentative smile at his clearly shell-shocked mate. "I look forward to getting to know you." Then he turned and walked back into the shop.

Rusty knew he was the center of attention, judging by the way the hairs on his neck stood on end, but he refused to look back.

CHAPTER TWO

"Wow." Acheron wasn't certain if he was angry, irritated, or heart-broken. After traveling North and South America for over eight decades, he'd finally run across his mate... and the man had practically run from him. "I... uh —"

Holy fucking shit! My mate, the other half of my soul, just blew me off!

A low growl escaped him.

Oh, hell no!

His frustration won out.

Before Acheron could figure out an appropriate response, he watched Adam offer him a commiserating smile before firing up the *Can-am* and driving the Spyder through an open chain-link gate.

"I don't know the cat shifter well, Acheron," Kontra told him, resting a hand on his neck and squeezing gently. "Perhaps Jethro can shed some light on Rusty's actions?"

"Uh... maybe..." Jethro began slowly. He'd shoved his hands into his pockets and rocked away from them a couple of steps. "Rusty is a very private, family oriented guy. Now, I don't have a shifter nose, but did any of you bother scenting him?" Shrugging, his expression uncomfortable, Jethro continued, "I'd say you embarrassed him by, well, not to be rude about it, coming onto him like a drunken prom queen."

"Or as if you were in a nightclub looking for a screw." Everyone turned to look at Lamar, whose brows were furrowed, and he sported a pinched look. "Rueben and I had a similar misunderstanding when we first met."

Rueben chuckled, nodding, as he wrapped his arm around Lamar's shoulders. "Yep, except I was the guy excited for what I thought was a hookup." Nuzzling Lamar's neck, he pressed a kiss to the peacock shifter's slender column of flesh. Rueben lowered his voice. "Took me a while to loosen ya up, and for me to come to terms with your need for more discretion, but we did it."

Acheron swallowed hard as he listened to the men's comments. He shoved his hands into his jacket pockets, fighting his desire to head into the store and track down his wayward mate. His scorpion had recognized the cat as being less dominant than himself, so even though he was the smaller of the pair, he craved the man's submission.

Hearing his scorpion chitter irritably in the back of his mind, Acheron took a step in that direction, pulling away from Kontra. He felt a hand clamp onto his shoulder, making him pause. While he managed to fight back a snarl, he still scowled. Seeing Kontra's narrow-eyed gaze, Acheron quickly cleared his throat... and his expression.

"Give your mate some space and learn from the experience," Kontra rumbled softly. "It will be easier the next time around."

Acheron blew out a harsh breath and allowed his eyelids to slide shut. Tipping his head back, he focused on enjoying the sun on his face. It had been a long time since he'd submitted to anyone, but he knew he needed to do it now.

Once Acheron felt calmer, he refocused on the grizzly shifter that he was trying to consider his alpha. "I know you're right." He let out a soft sigh, mentally shushing his irritated animal. "So, talking first." Acheron turned and focused on Jethro. "Guess I better get our paperwork done so you can pass on my phone number to him."

Jethro nodded. "Yeah. That's a good place to start."

With the reminder that he'd wandered for over a quarter

of a century looking for his mate, Acheron knew that in the grand scheme of things, another day wasn't going to hurt anything.

Yeah. Doesn't mean I have to like it.

"Haven't you ever heard the expression a watched pot never boils?"

Acheron lifted his gaze from his phone and peered at Sam Abbott. The big, broad, Texas longhorn shifter wore a concerned expression. There was a speculative gleam in his dark eyes.

"I was actually reading a book," Acheron told him, holding up his phone to display his open reading app. Although truth be told, he couldn't say what the last page had said. He waved at the seat across from him. "I'd be happy to have company, however."

Watching Sam ease into the large chair of the common room in the sprawling lodge-style home that Kontra's gang was renting, Acheron couldn't help noticing his tension. It didn't take a genius to realize what caused it. It wasn't the fact that Acheron had met his mate that day, either.

While Acheron's human form looked like a twink, his emperor scorpion was dominant—damn dominant. By the time he'd hit his fortieth year, he'd no longer been able to coax his animal into submitting to his alpha. It was either leave the nest or take it over.

Acheron had known there was no way that his shifter nest would accept a gay alpha. While the members of his old nest had whispered behind his ex-alpha's back about how horrible he was, that didn't mean they were progressive enough for *that* kind of change. Instead, Acheron had left.

He'd been on his own for almost one hundred years.

Kontra's people recognized the dominance of his animal, even when he wasn't trying to exert it. As the acknowledged beta of the gang, Sam definitely felt a little uneasy with him.

Sam wasn't the only one who didn't know how to treat him.

Even when I've done my best to keep a low profile. Oh, well. Looks like I may not be traveling with them anyway.

Setting his phone on the arm of the chair, Acheron kept his hand on it. He couldn't seem to get himself to let it go. Sam had been right that he was watching the clock.

"You've all been very kind to me," Acheron began slowly, softly, then he paused and scoffed. "Hell, you've been kinder to me and the humans you rescued than anyone I can think I've come across." Leveling a serious look at Sam, Acheron stated, "I'm not going to do anything around here to rock the boat. Please try to relax. I get that I'm an anomaly." Shrugging, he added, "Always have been. It's why I've been a loner for so long."

"That's going to change for you." Sam narrowed his eyes and leaned forward as he made the declaration. "You get that, right?"

Acheron tilted his head just a little as he shrugged. "Not really. Rusty is settled here, so here is where I need to stay. Jethro says Rusty doesn't have a pride." Staying in one place would definitely be a big change, though. Giving Sam a wry smile, he added, "Even though traveling with ya'll would have been fun." Acheron frowned, realizing the human boss probably didn't have all the facts. "At least, not one that he's aware of." Rubbing his face, he mused, "Although, Jethro did just learn about shifters not too long ago, and he said Rusty is pretty reserved. Maybe he just doesn't know about his pride?"

Gods above, that would totally suck.

Sam scoffed and shook his head. He leaned back in his chair, relaxing. "Actually, I'm reminding you that Rusty is a family man. He lives with his brother. That means you won't be alone." Sam's eyes narrowed as his lips curved into a hard smile. "Better accept that damn fast, Acheron."

"Rusty lives with his brother? Why?" Acheron had totally

missed that tidbit of information.

"Korvyn is confined to a wheelchair. I didn't hear why," Sam told him. "I met Korvyn once. He's a friendly, upbeat guy. They're definitely a package deal."

Frowning, Acheron blurted out, "You're not saying that Rusty is going to expect me to fuck Korvyn, too? Are you?" Just the idea caused him to cringe.

Sam barked a laugh, causing the scar bisecting his left cheek to crinkle in an interesting way.

Acheron used his focus on how the marred flesh appeared more jagged when the bull shifter laughed to keep his annoyance in check. He didn't appreciate being laughed at, even if his words sounded foolish when he had a chance to think about them. They were both shifters and fated mates.

No chance they'd be able to share.

Hearing Sam's chuckles easing, Acheron grumbled, "Yeah, yeah." He waved his hand, betraying his slight annoyance. "So, explain what you meant."

Sam's brown eyes continued to twinkle, but he nodded. "Very well. I mean you need to be prepared to win Korvyn's approval, or he could make things very difficult for you." Dipping his chin, Sam offered the warning with mirth in his tone, "Plus you might want to consider checking the thickness of Rusty's home's walls, seeing as the brothers live together."

Scoffing, Acheron couldn't help smirking back at the big male. "Hmmm, I've never heard of a shifter ending up in a wheelchair." He rubbed his thumb over his lips thoughtfully. "Do you know how it happened? Must have been a hell of an accident."

"Oh, Korvyn's not a shifter. He's human." Sam shook his head. "And I didn't hear how it happened or even what kind of paralysis it is. Not something you ask someone you only met a couple of times in passing."

Confusion filled him. "But you said they were brothers."

"Half-brothers," Sam amended. "Korvyn was the off-spring of their mother's first marriage, then she found a fated shifter mate, so—" As Sam grimaced, his expression turned a little vacant. "Can't imagine falling in love with someone, then having your world rocked by Fate and the existence of shifters. Must have been a hard change."

"I imagine so. Never been in a relationship myself," Acheron admitted. "Never been in one place long enough or found anyone interesting enough to give it a go."

That had all changed in the blink of an eye when he'd spotted the wiry, tawny-haired, bandana-wearing cat shifter admiring the Spyder Adam had driven. He'd wanted to get closer, to touch his lean, toned body. When he'd drawn nearer and he'd gotten his first whiff of the handsome male's scent, his fixation had immediately made complete sense.

Sidling up to the man and acting like a bitch cat in heat wasn't his finest moment. Still, he'd recognized that Rusty was a shifter. Shouldn't his mate have immediately responded, even if he was embarrassed?

None of the guys around them would have said much more than congratulations.

It was definitely something Acheron needed to find out.

I bet it was damn difficult for Lamar to speak out to me the way he did. Unless he's more dominant than I gave him credit for. The guy is pretty reserved.

"You know, it's okay to talk out your thoughts," Sam told him, cutting into his musings. He was smiling at him. "While I doubt you'll ever grow comfortable enough with any of us to do it, you should think about how to share with your mate." Leaning forward, Sam rested his forearms on his thick thighs. "Communication and compromise are a big part of making any mating work. You know that, right?"

Acheron swept his gaze over Sam's serious, earnest expression. While the advice, the warning, was unsolicited, he nodded anyway. He knew the other shifter was right.

Besides, the guy is in a stable, loving relationship with his human, I ought to take his advice.

"Thank you, Sam," Acheron began slowly. "I'll definitely give your words some thought, and I—"

The vibrating of the phone still under his hand cut him off.

Excitement surged through Acheron even before he'd moved his palm so he could look at the screen. Seeing Rusty's name and number on the screen—Jethro had given it to him with the express promise that he wouldn't call, but would wait for Rusty to make the first move—Acheron rose from his chair. "Thank you," he murmured to Sam as he hit the connect button and brought the phone to his ear. "This is Acheron."

"Good luck."

Acheron heard Sam's soft comment as he moved past him, intent on heading to his room. Just hearing Rusty's few words of greeting, "Hi, Acheron. This is Rusty," caused his blood to flow south. His cock swelled in his jeans, and he had to reach down and adjust himself so he didn't cut off circulation to his dick before climbing the stairs to the second story.

"Hi, Rusty."

Acheron just managed to cut off his comment about how just his mate's voice made him hard as nails. He wasn't used to curbing his tongue when he was interested in someone. Of course, in the past, that had always been in bars and clubs.

Jethro and Lamar had been right about that.

Instead, Acheron crooned, "I am so very happy to hear from you, Rusty."

Hearing a pause on the other end of the line, Acheron realized how suggestive just his tone might have seemed.

Gods, this is going to be difficult.

"Thank you for calling me," Acheron commented, trying again after he cleared his throat. He'd reached his room and slipped inside. Needing some way to start connecting, Acheron thought about Sam's words—communication and compromise. "I know we come from different worlds. Can we talk about that?"

Gotta start somewhere.

CHAPTER THREE

R usty sat on the seat of his Goldwing, his right foot on the foot peg and his left on the ground of his mechanic shop behind his home. The space was one area Korvyn rarely came unless Rusty asked him to. For his first conversation with his mate, he really wanted his privacy.

Just the man's tone had sounded like liquid sex, firing the blood in his veins. It'd caused his tongue to tie, and his mind blanked. He reached down and adjusted himself, then had to press the heel of his palm against the base of his prick to maintain control.

Did Acheron do that on purpose?

Hearing Acheron's next question spoken in a more serious tone, Rusty tried to get words out of his throat. "D-Different worlds?" His voice sounded rough even to his own ears, so he cleared his throat and tried again. "Yeah, I guess we should talk about that. What do you mean?"

Acheron hummed softly a moment. The sound of fabric rustling came through the line, making Rusty wonder what the man was doing.

"Well, I mean I am a one-hundred-thirty-two-year-old emperor scorpion shifter," Acheron told him, his voice taking on a quiet, musing quality. Wherever he was, it seemed he'd gotten comfortable. "I left my nest when I was forty, and I've been traveling ever since. Not all of those times were easy, since I look like a small black male, and I know I have a big personality. It matches my deep voice."

Acheron chuckled, and the husky sound went straight to

Rusty's balls, making them tingle.

"Anyway, I've been as far south as Buenos Aires, and I even spent around fifteen years living mostly in my scorpion form in the Amazon. That was an interesting time. I spent a few years in various locations in Canada, too, but I prefer heat to the cold, so I came back south. I was heading toward Texas when I was kidnapped by the biker gang." His tone darkened, and he growled softly. "I'd just woken when the gang came to move us, otherwise I would have found a way to escape. Kontra's people solved that problem for me, which I suppose is good." He sounded as if he were grumbling when he admitted, "I suppose they did a better job of helping all the humans than I could have, seeing as I am just one man."

With his mind reeling, Rusty didn't even know where to begin with all that information. His mate was older than him, which wasn't a surprise. Rusty was damn young for a shifter, only twenty-eight. He'd never traveled anywhere. He'd been too busy caring for his family, since his mother and brother's injuries.

Should he admit those things?

Guess I better.

"Rusty?" Acheron murmured softly. "Did I overload you?" A deep sigh came through the line. "I admit I'm not good at this. Please say something."

Getting his head out of his ass, Rusty did just that. "Yeah, a little bit," he answered honestly. His mate was obviously trying in some awkward way to share things about himself. Rusty needed to do the same. "Uh, so... guess I should warn you that you're definitely right. Totally different worlds." Rubbing his free hand over his thigh, he told the man, "I'm twenty-eight, so I actually look my age. I have a human mother and a shifter father. My brother, uh, half-brother, Korvyn, he's human."

When Rusty paused, Acheron commented, "Wow,

twenty-eight." He chuckled softly before saying, "Guess that makes sense. Sam told me Korvyn lives with you and you care for him."

Rusty racked his mind, then it clicked. "Sam. Kontra's beta?"

"Yeah."

Having met the Texas longhorn bull shifter a couple of times, had even gone with the group on a motorcycle ride where he'd taken Korvyn, he couldn't help but smile. "Kontra's group are busybodies. Did you notice?"

Acheron rumbled a low snicker. "Yeah. Yeah, I have. They mean well."

"True, although not always on the up and up," Rusty countered. "I've heard how they've done some underhanded things to keep their people safe or remove a danger from their pack."

"Uh, I don't actually have a problem with that," Acheron told him. "I mean, I'm one of the people they helped by doing something underhanded. Did you know that while they stopped the head buyer's right-hand man, the guy he answered to is still at large? They know his name is Wayland Davidson, and that he runs a bunch of shady business dealings out of Chicago, but his actual address is unlisted. He's a danger to me, and if I see him, I don't have any issue with turning into my scorpion and stinging him."

The revelation of the danger that Acheron was bringing to not only Rusty, but his family, caused his gut to clench and his arousal to wane—and it wasn't just from the shifter's choice of wheels. At least his cock no longer throbbed. Still, it was definitely something that he needed to consider.

"You're my mate, though," Rusty whispered. "I—" He brought his free hand to his face and rubbed it over his eyes. "Shit."

"Rusty, what—Ah, I see." Acheron's tone took on a soothing quality. "You just realized mating with me comes with a certain measure of danger."

Acheron paused for a second, but it wasn't long enough for Rusty to do much more than grunt in confirmation.

"Life is risk, my young mate." Acheron once more crooned, his voice turning husky. "We have no guarantee of tomorrow. While we can plan for the future, we must seize each day and recognize it for the gift that it is. My sweet kitty, I'd very much like to start doing that with you sooner rather than later."

Rusty had to acknowledge the truth of Acheron's words. His cat yowled softly in the back of his mind, wanting to do as the man on the other end of the line encouraged. Knowing his mate was a more dominant shifter than himself, even though he was much smaller, would take some getting used to.

"I know," Rusty whispered. "I agree, too." After a second of hesitation, he explained, "My mother and my brother were hit by a drunk driver twelve years ago. Korvyn is two years my senior. I was sixteen at the time. He was eighteen." Scoffing softly, he recalled the anger and fear his brother had worked through. "My mother physically came out of it fairly well, but still harbors guilt, even though the accident was in no way her fault. The other guy ran a red light and t-boned my mother's vehicle on Korvyn's side."

"I'm sorry that happened to your family." Acheron actually sounded as if he meant it, too. "I haven't seen or spoken to my family since I left. We weren't exactly what you'd call... loving."

"That's too bad." Rusty couldn't imagine living without his family, even when times had been tough. They'd all supported each other. "Family is important."

"That is... something I hope to learn about."

Rusty opened his mouth, then closed it again. He had no

clue how to respond to Acheron's comment. The man's im-
plication was clear, though—he wanted to learn about it
from Rusty.

"You mentioned going for a meal."

Appreciating the subject change, Rusty latched onto the
new topic. "Yes. Yes, I did. Uh—" He thought quickly.
"What kind of food do you like? There are a few really good
choices in town."

"Actually, I was hoping for something a little more se-
cluded," Acheron told him. "You may have noticed I'm a
dominant shifter. Keeping my hands off of you..." He ended
on a hum. "When I see something I want, I'm not a patient
man, Rusty." A soft growling sound came through the line,
the sound one of discontent. "I'll try to give you time, but—
gods, Rusty. You're my mate. You're a shifter, too. Surely
you understand?"

Rusty *did* understand. His cat had been grumbling un-
happily in his mind all afternoon.

"Yeah." Whispering the word, Rusty rubbed at his temples. "What, uh, what did you have in mind?"

"May I come over tomorrow evening and grill for you?"
Acheron hesitated, then added, "For both you and Korvyn?"

Rusty's knee-jerk reaction was to accept. He took a few
heartbeats to think about that, however. "You want to meet
Korvyn right away?"

"I do." Acheron sounded adamant. "Korvyn is your
brother. He is a big part of your life. I think we need to meet
immediately. Wait. Does Korvyn know about shifters?"

"Yeah," Rusty assured, waylaying that concern. "He
knows about us. That's not an issue."

"And does he know about fated mates and our swift need
to bond?"

At the very mention of bonding, Rusty's breath caught in
his throat. He felt a shiver of need travel down his spine. His

blood heated, and his nipples pebbled.

Rusty must have let out some noise betraying his arousal, for Acheron moaned roughly. "Oh, my sexy kitty. The sounds I want to ring from your body." He growled through the line, possessive and low. "We will have such bliss together."

A groan ripped from Rusty before he could stifle the noise.

"Yessss," Acheron hissed. "You do like the sound of that."

Pressing the heel of his hand to the base of his prick again, Rusty blurted, "I-I've never been with a man."

Of course, he'd only been with a few women, too, but he didn't reveal that.

"Rusty." Acheron seemed to speak his name as if it was a prayer. "That knowledge." He grunted, and the sound of clothes rustling came through the line. "Do you have any idea how close I am to getting off right now?"

Gasping upon hearing Acheron's confession, Rusty palmed himself through his jeans. His balls tingled and rolled. Pre-cum dampened the inside of his fly. Even his cat purred in his head.

"What about you, Rusty?" Acheron growled his name. "Are you close, too? Does talking to me, hearing my voice turn you on as much as yours does to me?" Chuckling huskily, he asked, "If I tell you how I want to straddle your lap and grind my dick against yours, how I want to wrap my hands around us both as I writhe on your lap, spreading our scents all over each other, does that make your balls ache?"

Rusty whimpered, yanking open his fly. "Yes," he responded breathlessly. He wrapped his fingers around his throbbing erection, desperate for stimulation. "Oh fuck!"

"Oh, we will." Acheron's moan sounded in Rusty's ear. "Damn, that feels better. So fucking hard for you, Rusty. I'm stroking myself for you, babe. Are you gonna rub one out for me, too?"

Leaning back, Rusty rested his head against the passenger seat's backrest. He planted his second foot on the floor and began rocking into his touch. Moans and whimpers escaped him as heat suffused his body.

Rusty felt his balls tighten as an image of Acheron lying on a bed touching himself entered his mind.

"Gods, those are sexy sounds," Acheron mumbled. "Gonna come from listening to you pleasure yourself, Rusty."

Unable to form a thought in his head, Rusty mindlessly jacked himself as he listened to Acheron's sexy croonings. He didn't know how the man could still talk, but he sounded so good, telling him what he was doing, jacking his dick, playing with his foreskin, and teasing his frenulum. He interspersed that with the huskiest of rumbles, grunts, and growls.

"I might be dominant, but I'm a switch, babe," Acheron continued. "But I'll still be in charge. I can't wait to tie your hands to the bedposts and ride your dick. My ass will squeeze you so good while I'm bouncing on you, taking you nice and slow, then fast and hard. Maybe I'll sit on your groin and play with myself, not letting you come until I've sprayed my seed all over your chest, coating you in my scent."

Rusty could no longer fight his body's need. As the image of Acheron's lithe black body sitting on him, spraying him, filled his mind, he imaged that the squeeze of his fist was his mate's rectum. His balls pulled tight, and he roared as his cock pulsed.

As Rusty flew on the endorphin release, hard trembles racking his body, he vaguely felt the warmth of his seed soaking his shirt. He recognized Acheron's rough shout of completion and grinned at the ceiling.

"Wow," Rusty croaked, still trying to catch his breath.

That was unexpected.

Acheron hummed, the sound one of sated contentment. "Is that a yes?" he asked, his own voice husky. "Can I come see you tomorrow? Feed you?"

"Yeah." The word was out of Rusty's mouth before he could think better of it. Even if his brain had been on-line, he wouldn't have been able to deny his mate. Not now. "Tomorrow."

"Yes, Rusty. Tomorrow. I look forward to it."

As they confirmed a time then said their goodbyes — Rusty promising to text his address — he didn't think the next eighteen hours could go by fast enough.

CHAPTER FOUR

"Remember to be patient," Yuma told Acheron, who was strapping the soft-sided lunch cooler to the back of his bike.

Acheron finished, then glanced the small penguin shifter's way. "Of course." He'd try, anyway.

Hearing Rusty's response to just his words and tone had made resisting the impulse to go to his mate the evening before extremely tough. Phone sex with Rusty had given him the best damn orgasm... that he could ever remember. He desperately wanted to top it.

"Knowing when to push is just as important as offering time," Adam warned as he hip-checked Noah. "Right, mate?"

Noah's cheeks took on a rosy hue, but he nodded.

"And conversation requires more than one person talking," Sam reminded him. "Listen as well."

Nodding, Acheron placed his helmet on his head and swung onto the bike. "I'll do my best." He focused on the beta and gave him a wry smile. "But I'm still learning."

"Well, just give him multiple orgasms then." Payson waggled his brows as he spoke his suggestion. "That makes everything better."

Snorting, Acheron shook his head and fired up his Ninja.

"They mean well." Kontra stopped beside the bike and held out a leather jacket.

Taking it, Acheron felt that it was a style with hard plastic shielding inside the lining. He lifted a brow. A leather jacket was hot enough on a warm spring evening, which was why he hadn't bothered to put one on. Besides, he was a shifter.

Obviously seeing the question in his eyes, Kontra smiled. "Wear it. Trust me. Your mate will appreciate your nod to safety."

"Ah..." Acheron mused as he shrugged into the jacket. The helmet and protective style jacket would make it seem as if he cared for his safety, even while zipping around on a motorcycle built for speed. "Thank you."

"Sure, and good luck."

"And don't try to make out in front of Korvyn," Lamar called, waving. His lips curved into a slight smirk. "While Rusty might enjoy the kiss, he'll feel embarrassed about it later."

Acheron nodded again. "Again, thank you."

That was definitely something he'd have to remember, because it never would have occurred to him.

Putting his motorcycle into gear, Acheron headed away from the group of shifters and their mates, eagerly making his way in the direction of his own waiting man.

As Acheron drove, he thought about what he'd learned the evening before. Rusty had no experience with men. That knowledge got him hotter than he would have expected. For some reason, Acheron loved the idea of teaching his mate from the ground up. The possessiveness was an unexpected feeling.

Following Rusty's directions, Acheron easily located his mate's home. It was on a country road that offered decent seclusion. The lots were large, offering generous amounts of space between homes. There were plenty of trees, too, as it appeared there was a stream running behind some of the homes.

The tree cover on Rusty's spread appeared exceptionally thick, which didn't surprise Acheron. The man would need privacy to shift and play. Not for the first time, Acheron wondered what kind of cat shifter his mate was.

Hopefully, I'll find out soon.

Stopping his bike before the two car garage, Acheron noticed a short wheelchair ramp leading to the front door of the ranch-style home. There were also two steps on the front of the extra-wide porch, although a number of leaves littered them, betraying that they probably weren't used much. A gravel drive went around the back of the home, and he wondered what was back there and looked forward to exploring his mate's territory. It would also give him time to confirm that there were no poisonous snakes or spiders in the vicinity of Rusty or Korvyn.

Yep, I can help around here in small ways.

Acheron took off his helmet and swung off the bike, then placed the headgear on the fuel tank. After unhooking the lunch bag, he headed toward the front door. He'd offered to bring drinks, but his mate had declined, assuring him that he had several options that would go with steak.

By the time Acheron reached the door, he noticed that it'd been opened. He spotted a black-haired man in a wheelchair waiting for him. The guy had a speculative expression on his face as he openly perused Acheron, but at least he sported a smile.

"Hi," Acheron greeted, holding out his hand. "Korvyn, is it?"

Korvyn nodded and took his hand. "That's me."

Acheron gave the man's hand a firm shake, then released him. "I'm Acheron. Can I assume Rusty told you I was coming?"

Gripping his wheels, Korvyn backed his chair. "Yeah, come on in. Rusty's in the shower. That's the water running you hear." He waved a hand toward the left side of the house and the hallway there, which was opposite the open concept floor plan. "I'm sure he won't be long. He probably heard your bike over the sound of the water. Take off your boots and join me in the kitchen. What'd you bring?"

Acheron found the human's open welcome interesting. *Would the questions come later?* As soon as he sat down on the boot box and began unbuckling his boots, he got his answer.

"So, mates, huh?"

Glancing up once before returning his attention to his boots, Acheron nodded. "Yeah. Your brother is my mate." He straightened on the boot box so he could focus on the other man as he toed off his footwear. "I hope we can come to some kind of friendship, Korvyn," he stated honestly. "Because I'm not going anywhere."

Korvyn grinned widely, waggling his brows. "Does that mean you're going to sneak me beer and stuff?"

Acheron opened his mouth, then snapped it shut again. He had no desire to do anything that would upset his mate, even to get in the man's brother's good graces. Acheron mentally scrambled for how to respond to the grinning male.

"You don't need to sneak beer," Rusty grumbled, appearing from the hallway across the room. "Don't make my mate feel like he has to do something wrong just so you won't give him shit about us."

Sweeping his gaze over his approaching mate, Acheron nearly swallowed his tongue. In grease-stained jeans and a work shirt, Rusty had been handsome enough. Wearing a pair of khaki shorts and a pale green polo shirt that set off his honey-brown eyes—*stunning!*

"Aww, I was just giving him shit, Rusty," Korvyn replied, wheeling backward a little and turning, so he could look his brother's way. "It's part of the deal. He mates with you, becomes your husband, that means I'm his brother-in-law." He snickered, clearly finding the situation humorous. "That means I have a free pass to give him a hard time."

Acheron remembered the gang's warnings and yanked

his gaze back to Korvyn. He processed the human's words. *"Huh." That'll take some getting used to.* "I suppose there are worse things."

"There. See?" Korvyn laughed. "Acheron doesn't mind." He swatted Acheron with the back of his hand, then turned his chair and began wheeling toward the dining room. "I'm gonna get a beer. Want one? And what's in the bag?"

Thoroughly confused on how to respond, Acheron cocked his head as he glanced between the pair. He finally rested his gaze on Rusty and lifted both brows. It didn't escape his notice that his mate's cheeks had a pinkish hue to them.

"Uh, sorry I wasn't out earlier," Rusty murmured, stopping a couple feet in front of him and shoving his hands in his pockets. "Got off work a little later than I'd hoped, then got distracted by — " His cheeks darkened further. "Anyway, we should probably head to the kitchen."

Acheron rose to his sock-clad feet and picked up his lunch duffel. "I understand kissing is supposed to be done at the end of the date, and I was warned not to try to make out with you in front of your brother." Closing the distance between them, he noticed the instant that tension tightened Rusty's shoulders, so he stopped with about eight inches between them. "But I do still very much want to touch." Lifting his free hand, he reached toward Rusty's torso, pausing when his fingertips were a couple of inches from his shirt. "May I?"

Rusty's nostrils flared, and a tremble worked through his body. His mouth opened and closed, and his eyes dilated.

"Please say yes," Acheron urged.

Slowly, Rusty dipped his chin in a slight nod.

Pleased, Acheron rested his hand on Rusty's pectoral. He smoothed his hand upward, being careful to avoid his nipple. The contact wasn't meant to stimulate so much as forge a connection between them.

That didn't mean Acheron missed the smooth, hard lines of his body. Reaching Rusty's shoulder, he squeezed the tendon lightly as he scraped his thumb along the pulse point in his neck. His mouth watered as he thought about sinking his canines into his mate's flesh and marking him.

"Thank you for having me over, Rusty," Acheron murmured, holding his mate's gaze. "I look forward to getting to know you."

Rusty licked his lips, then swallowed hard enough that his Adam's apple bobbed. Lifting his hand, he laid it over Acheron's wrist. He gripped him lightly. When Rusty urged him to release his shoulder and rotate his wrist, Acheron didn't fight him on it. As his mate nuzzled his nose along the inside of his wrist, Acheron's blood heated, and the hairs on his nape stood on end.

Oh, fuck yeah. My mate is marking me.

Peering at him from beneath his lashes, betraying not only his pleasure but his submission, Rusty smiled at him. "Me, too. Very much." His cheeks darkened further, causing the color to spread down his neck. Rusty cleared his throat, then stepped away from him. "So, uh, come on back, and we'll get that drink, and I'll show you where the grill is."

Acheron lowered his hand as he nodded. When Rusty turned and headed deeper into the home, he slid his gaze over his mate's wiry form, pausing at the man's rounded ass. He wanted to close the distance between them and grip those globes, to squeeze and rub and see if they were as hard as they looked.

"Acheron?"

Yanking his focus upward, Acheron met Rusty's gaze. He saw his shifter's lifted brow and realized he'd been caught looking. Acheron shrugged as he got himself moving.

"Sorry," Acheron murmured, then rolled his eyes. "Not really. I'm actually sorry you caught me and it made you uncomfortable."

Rusty's lips curved, and a soft chuckle escaped him. "Please don't apologize for looking at me like that, especially in my home. I'm just—" His cheeks remained flushed as he rested his hand on the kitchen counter and tapped his fingertips on it restlessly. Finally, he mumbled, "Just not used to it."

"Ah." Acheron slid the fingertips of his free hand across Rusty's back as he passed him, rounding the bar and moving into the kitchen. "Then I will endeavor to change that."

Deciding a subject change was in order, Acheron placed the bag on the counter and unzipped it. "I need a cookie sheet or platter. Something to spread the meat out on." He pointed at the contents. "There are several slabs of ribs marinating as well as a couple of steaks." Acheron turned his attention to Korvyn, who was just rolling back into the kitchen through a door that led to a large utility room. "You do eat meat, right? I asked about allergies, but probably should have confirmed that you're not a vegetarian."

Korvyn grinned widely. "Yeah, I eat meat." He waggled his brows. "I even gave Rusty some pointers last night about eating meat when he told me about you."

"Fuck! Korvyn!"

Laughing, Korvyn grinned. "What? I was just trying to help you be comfortable doing just that."

"That's the last thing—"

Acheron scented Rusty's shock, heard his cry, even as his own brows lifted. Anger surged through him, but he squelched it. His initial reaction was to snarl at the man who was upsetting his mate. Except, this was his brother, so he knew he couldn't.

Clearing his throat, Acheron drew attention to himself. He grinned widely at Korvyn, holding the cheeky human's gaze as he leaned against the counter. "While I appreciate your attempts at assistance, I plan to take *great* pleasure in teaching Rusty everything he needs to know." Acheron winked, gratified to see a slight pinkish hue creeping over Korvyn's cheeks. "*Everything.*"

Once Korvyn's brows had lifted and his lips had parted, his shock perfuming the air, Acheron turned and looked at the food. "So." He peered at Rusty, offering a reassuring smile. "How about that platter?"

To his relief, Rusty cleared his throat and jerked a nod. He headed around the counter and opened a cupboard, clearly happy to move on.

CHAPTER FIVE

R usty felt like his heart would pound right out of his chest. Both arousal and embarrassment warred within him. He couldn't believe Korvyn's antics, and Acheron's actions were just as confusing.

After grabbing a cookie sheet from a lower cabinet, Rusty straightened and turned. His breath caught. Taking in Acheron's warm regard, he felt his blood heat for a new reason.

My mate's goal was to stop Korvyn from saying anything else that would embarrass me. That was very kind of him.

"H-Here you go."

"Thank you." Acheron took the item and placed it on the counter. "So, got a favorite barbeque sauce in the house?" he asked, turning his attention to carefully easing the pieces of meat out of the resealable bags inside the soft-sided lunch case. "If not, I brought some." Acheron pointed at a bottle tucked underneath. He then glanced over his shoulder at Korvyn. "And how about that beer? Plus, why would you make a joke about me sneaking you some if you have it in the house?"

Korvyn's scoff yanked Rusty out of his admiration of his short, lean mate. "Um, yeah, yeah." Rusty turned toward his brother. "We have a local favorite. Grab it from the fridge when you get those beers, huh?"

"Uh, sure. Yeah." Korvyn turned his chair and opened the fridge.

Slipping between Acheron and his brother's chair, Rusty couldn't resist sliding his hand along the smaller shifter's neck. He took a second to admire the differences between his bronzed flesh and his mate's much darker tone. Touching the divot at the base of the neck caused Acheron to hum softly as he offered him a pleased-looking side-eyed glance.

"Korvyn does take certain meds, so there is a limit to how much alcohol he can have on any given day," Rusty told him softly, unable to pull his hand away. Acheron's skin was just too smooth. Plus, his mate didn't seem to mind. "While we have beer in the house, we don't drink it much." Furrowing his brows, he added, "Especially in lieu of how Korvyn ended up in that chair."

"Ah." Acheron's lips curved into a wry smile. "A test." He glanced Korvyn's way before focusing on the food again. "To see how sensitive I'd be to you and your brother's needs. Interesting." After he completed laying out the meat, Acheron straightened and met Rusty's gaze. "I'm not familiar with family rituals. Did I pass?"

"Yeah, you passed," Rusty assured quietly, smiling at his mate. Realizing he still teased his fingertips over the back of Acheron's neck, he pulled his hand away and grinned. "You started the grill, then?"

Holding out his hand for the pair of beers Korvyn was holding out, Rusty watched him nod.

"Yeah. It's warming," Korvyn told him before reaching into the fridge to grab a drink of his own, choosing bottled iced tea. "Hey, what kind of steak is that?"

"Are you asking if it's something other than beef?" Acheron asked, turning and taking the barbeque sauce that Korvyn had grabbed along with his tea. Glancing at the label, he added, "Oh, spicy. Nice. Nothing wrong with a bit of zing on the meat." Acheron glanced at Rusty and winked, then asked, "Basting brush?"

"Yeah. Is it cow? Or some other exotic meat?" Korvyn rolled across the kitchen, barking a laugh. "You know that's how Rusty got me to eat moose. Didn't tell me. Just plopped a slab of grilled meat on my plate."

Acheron's lips curved into a half-smile as he met Rusty's gaze. His dark eyes twinkled. "I'll remember that trick."

Placing the one beer bottle on the counter and popping the cap off the second, Rusty grinned back at Acheron. "Well, he'd turned it down at our parents' house the week before, and I told him he was missing out. He'd glibly responded, *bet not.*" Winking at Acheron, he placed the beer close to his mate, then picked up the second and opened that, too. "I won that bet."

"Oh, yeah?" Acheron took the brush from Korvyn, then set it on the tray. "So. What'd you win?"

Rusty opened his mouth, then paused. His cheeks heated a little. He exchanged a glance with Korvyn and saw his brother's lips twitch.

Acheron turned to the sink and quickly washed his hands. Then he picked up the beer and moved to stand in the space between the kitchen and dining room. After he'd taken a sip of his drink, Acheron rested his forearms on the bar. A soft chuckle escaped him as he glanced between them.

"Wow. Good story?" Acheron's lips twitched. "Or embarrassing story?"

While Rusty continued to struggle for a few seconds, Korvyn offered, "Hey, you brought it up." His dark eyes twinkled as he offered the mental jab, "What? Hiding your vices until later in the relationship?"

"Vices?" Acheron's brows shot up, and his eyes widened. "Are vices normally shared on the first date?"

"You're mates. Is this actually a date?" Korvyn asked pointedly.

Rusty cleared his throat. "When Korvyn lost the bet, he had to eat anchovy and spinach pizza with me."

Acheron's jaw sagged open. His expression one of clear

shock. For an instant, he just stared.

"Anchovies and spinach... on a pizza?"

Holding Acheron's gaze, Rusty nodded. "I think it must be the cat in me. I love all fish."

"What kind of cat are you, anyway?"

"I'm a serval cat. The non-shifter variety hale from the African plains." Seeing Acheron's narrowed eyes and scenting his confusion, Rusty explained, "If some unknowing human spotted me out running, they might mistake me for a very small leopard, but my legs are longer and my ears are larger."

"I would love to see that, my se-sweet mate."

Seeing the way Acheron glanced discreetly at Korvyn, Rusty just knew that he had amended what he was going to say. He could probably guess, since his mate had already called him sexy on more than one occasion. His response to such a compliment—his chest warming and the feel of butterflies in his stomach—was far more confusing.

"I run often," Rusty told him. "I'm sure it'll happen soon enough."

"Good." Acheron took a sip of his beer. "Well, in the spirit of sharing vices, I have a hell of a time remembering to put the toilet seat down." He shrugged, twirling the beer between his fingertips. "Good thing you're not a girl, eh?"

For a second, Rusty's mind blanked. When Korvyn barked a laugh and stated, "Stay out of my bathroom, then." He waved at himself. "I don't stand to pee, so—"

Acheron's lips parted, and he darted a glance between them. "Oh, shit. Right." Grimacing, he mumbled, "That was thoughtless of me. Sorry."

"Don't sweat it." Korvyn grinned broadly. With the way his eyes creased, Rusty knew he wasn't the least bit upset. "Hell, it's kinda nice that you'd forget such a thing. Ya know?"

Nodding slowly, Acheron shifted from foot to foot, still appearing uncertain.

In an effort to reassure, Rusty reached over and touched his upper arm, teasing along the flesh until his fingers dipped under his sleeve. Immediately, Acheron's focus snapped to him, and his eyelids lowered to half-mast. He slipped out his tongue and slid it over his bottom lip.

The heady smell of Acheron's arousal flooded the space around them. Rusty's own body responded. His blood heated and flowed south. Staring into Acheron's hungry gaze, Rusty slid his hand around and gripped his mate's bicep with the intention of pulling his mate closer so he could smell him better.

"Aaaaand, I'm gonna go check on the grill," Korvyn cut in, mirth in his tone. "I'd say you should head out and cook, that way you could make out on the back deck"—he started rolling his wheelchair back through the mudroom—"but I'd be afraid you'd burn the meat, and I really want some of those ribs."

With that parting shot, accompanied by a few snorts of laughter, Korvyn left.

"Shit, I'm sorry," Acheron murmured before blowing out a harsh breath. He peered in the direction Korvyn had disappeared, then back at Rusty. "Lamar warned me that coming onto you in front of Korvyn would embarrass your brother." Waving his hand, he added, "And by extension, you. That wasn't my intention." Rubbing his lifted hand over his closely buzzed black hair, he muttered, "You're just—your touch is—"

After glancing toward the mudroom again, Acheron met Rusty's gaze fully. "I have another vice. Sex." The next look that he swept over Rusty was so hungry it felt almost like a physical caress. "I've been enjoying sex since I was fourteen—the endorphin release, the physical contact, the give and take of pleasure." For a second, Acheron's eyes glazed a little, and a shudder worked through his body. He blinked once, twice, then refocused on Rusty as he wrapped his free hand back around his beer bottle. "Having my mate near and not acting is... a strange sort of torture."

Rusty felt a surge of anger mixed with jealousy. For an instant, he tightened his hold on Acheron's arm. Then the image of Acheron with his arm around Louis entered his mind.

Growling low in his throat, Rusty fisted his hands as he glared at Acheron. "Were you going to have sex with Louis?" he demanded, his voice rising with every word he spoke. "Were you going to fuck him? Is that why you were holding him? Were you seducing him?"

Acheron's eyes narrowed just a little, then widened. His dark eyes seemed to spark with a light of their own. "If you must know, no, I wasn't, not that it has any relevance on us."

"What the hell do you mean it doesn't have relevance on us?" Rusty couldn't remember the last time he'd felt such jealous anger. "You're my mate. Of course, it matters. Everything you do matters to me!"

His nostrils flaring, Acheron straightened and took the step around the counter. He boldly entered Rusty's personal space and gripped his upper arms in a tight hold. Tipping his head back, he scowled up at him.

"You're attempting to cause a fight, and I don't know why."

The snarl in Acheron's tone made Rusty's cat uneasy. He swallowed hard, trying to understand the riot of emotions coursing through him. While Rusty still felt jealousy, it eased to a simmer. The close proximity of Acheron, the feel of his hands on his skin, caused Rusty to feel a wave of heat of another kind.

"Explain."

Clenching his jaw, Rusty fought against his more dominant mate's command. Hell, he didn't know what to say anyway. His mood swings were... he didn't understand himself.

Acheron slid his hands up Rusty's arms. Resting one on his neck, he massaged his nape lightly. He moved the second into Rusty's hair, using the hold to tip his head, forcing him to bare his throat.

Rusty sighed, relaxing in the smaller man's hold. He didn't scent any anger or annoyance from his mate. His cat purred in his mind at the petting sensations, and he lowered his eyelids to half-mast as he enjoyed the feelings his mate caused.

"Can you talk to me, my sexy kitty?" Acheron murmured soothingly. "Tell me what riled you."

Finding his tongue, Rusty whispered, "I didn't like hearing you talk about sex with others." He growled at his own words. "You're *my* mate."

"What we've done before meeting each other must be dismissed," Acheron declared. "I'm a lot older than you, but neither of us are virgins, even if you haven't ever been with a man." His tone changed, becoming husky. "Although that *is* something I intend to change... soon."

Swallowing hard, Rusty jerked a nod. He knew Acheron was right. Knowing it and getting his tumultuous emotions under control were two very different things.

CHAPTER SIX

Acheron wanted to drag Rusty into the living room, shove him down on the sofa, and ravish him. Too bad he knew that wasn't an option, and it wasn't just because Korvyn could return at any second. They really needed to talk about what had just happened.

Petting the man certainly seemed to calm him down. Acheron figured that was the cat in Rusty. He continued to gently scratch his scalp and massage his nape for a good thirty seconds.

That also gave Acheron a chance to cool his raging libido.

Easing his hands away from Rusty took more self-control than Acheron thought he had left, but he managed it. He smiled up at his cat shifter. Seeing the relaxed expression on his face, he decided he'd waited long enough to see what he tasted like.

Acheron rested his right hand on Rusty's shoulder. Rising onto his toes, he pressed his lips to his mate's. He felt the man's lips part as he heard Rusty gasp. Taking advantage, Acheron teased his tongue into the other shifter's mouth.

Exploring Rusty, Acheron enjoyed the masculine flavor of the man he hoped to soon make his lover. He slid their appendages together, tasting him fully. His natural dark essence seemed mixed with something minty.

Toothpaste.

Feeling Rusty's hands land on his hips and his fingers tighten, Acheron knew they could get out of control so very swiftly. When he eased the kiss to an end, separating them,

Rusty moaned and tried to chase his lips. Loving that response, Acheron almost gave in.

The outer door banging reminded Acheron why they couldn't.

Grinning up at Rusty, Acheron murmured, "You taste amazing, my mate."

"Y-You, too," Rusty replied breathlessly, his honey-brown eyes dark with arousal. "Maybe we should skip dinner."

Acheron groaned as he eased a step away from Rusty. "I love that idea very much, Rusty, but is it truly what you want?" If he answered yes, Acheron would take him up on it in a heartbeat, but he sort of knew better. "Or are your shifter hormones and urges messing with you as much as mine are with me?"

Grimacing, Rusty turned and rested his fisted hands on the bar. He bowed his head.

That was answer enough for Acheron. Rounding the counter, he picked up the cookie sheet turned tray and offered, "Let's see if that grill is ready."

Rusty nodded and headed past him, leading the way.

Once again, Acheron found himself enjoying the view of Rusty's ass. He really wanted to tap the bigger man's gorgeous globes. His desire to drive his mate out of his mind with pleasure caused a bead of pre-cum to ooze from his aching dick.

Damn. Being responsible sucks... and not in the way I love.

With that thought, Acheron recalled Rusty's response to his vice admission. Something occurred to him. "It seems we found a second vice of yours, my mate."

Rusty opened the door that led to an expansive back deck. Holding the door open for Acheron, he paused and lifted one brow. "Huh?" He cleared his throat, then added, "What do you mean?"

Acheron fought back a chuckle. It seemed that his mate's ability to think clearly definitely went out the window when he was aroused. Acheron planned to take advantage of that tidbit of information.

"Well, you jump to conclusions a little too quickly," Acheron told him, forcing himself to stick with the conversation. "You did it at the shop, too, when we first met."

Rusty's cheeks flushed as he closed the door. When he turned back to face him, he nodded. "It's something I've always tried to work on." His lips twisting in a crooked smile, Rusty mumbled, "Guess I'm still not very good at it."

Acheron carefully balanced the tray on one hand so he could place his other on Rusty's upper arm. Squeezing lightly, he stood on his toes again and pressed a kiss to his cheek. Immediately, he saw his mate's eyelids lower to half-mast.

Yep, my man certainly responds to me damn fast.

"You work on that," Acheron whispered. "And I'll work on putting the toilet seat down." Rusty's eyes widened, and Acheron grinned at him. "Don't want to piss off Korvyn, after all."

As Rusty began to nod, the man in question piped up, "Then how about we get this show on the road? The grill's been ready for ten minutes."

Laughing at the wheelchair-bound man's impetuous attitude, Acheron nodded and pulled away from Rusty. He crossed to the grill and got to work.

Acheron cooked the meat to perfection, in his opinion, removing the steaks first. While he'd done that, Korvyn and Rusty had set the outdoor table they had on the deck. They'd added more drinks as well as a cheesy pasta salad, a green salad, and mashed potatoes and gravy.

Rusty stayed in the kitchen to make the gravy fresh, while Korvyn made plenty of trips in and out to get dishes and silverware. Each time he'd returned, he had asked another question. Mostly they'd been about the places Acheron traveled, which he was happy to answer.

Once they'd all sat down, Korvyn asked, "So, are you moving in right away?" He grinned cheekily as he waggled his brows. "I'd tell you that you have to keep it down, but I sleep with earplugs and an *iPod* anyway. You can make as much noise as you want."

While Rusty growled Korvyn's name, the brother laughed.

Acheron decided to answer honestly. "I haven't had a place I called home in decades." He reached out and gripped Rusty's wrist, rubbing his thumb over the back of his hand. "I would very much like to move in immediately, but that will be up to your brother."

Seeing Rusty's gaping, wide-eyed look, Acheron shrugged. He squeezed once, then released him, returning his attention to his fall-off-the-bone ribs.

"Uh, y-yeah." Rusty cut into his steak, giving Acheron a side-eyed look. "You're my mate, so, um... you can move in right away. That's the way we do it." His brows furrowed as he met Korvyn's gaze. "If that's okay with you? This is your home, too, so you do have a say in it."

Korvyn snorted. "As if I'd ever try to keep you away from your mate." After popping a bite of steak into his mouth, he said around his mouthful, "O' course ya can move in, 'specially if ya're goin' ta keep grillin' like this." Without missing a beat, he swallowed and continued, "So, whadda ya do for work?"

"Gods, don't talk with your mouth full," Rusty grumbled, rolling his eyes. "We can hardly understand anything you just said."

"Saw'ree," Korvyn muttered, still chewing.

Acheron chuckled softly, unable to help himself. He couldn't remember the last time he'd enjoyed a family meal. Focusing on Korvyn, who was shoving another big piece of steak into his mouth, he grinned widely.

"You asked earlier what kind of steak it is, and it really is cow. Ribeyes." Turning his attention to Rusty, Acheron crooned, "Only the best for my mate." He scooped up a spoonful of the cheesy pasta salad as he added, "The ribs are pork, so best of both worlds. As for work, odd jobs mostly. I've lived half my life hitch-hiking and moving around, the other half as my emperor scorpion, which doesn't need money." Shrugging, he added, "I could shift, eat a bunch of bugs, then shift back, so even food and shelter didn't need to be paid for." Knowing he'd never be happy living off his mate, Acheron sighed. "Guess I'll take a look in town and see who's hiring."

Acheron slid the food into his mouth, humming appreciatively. "Good," he murmured after he'd chewed and swallowed.

"I work part-time at the library," Korvyn told him. "They have a board where job openings are posted. You want me to check it out for you?"

"Yeah." Acheron slid his knife through the meat of the pork ribs, separating them. "Thank you."

"And thank you for this meat," Rusty commented. "It really is amazing."

As Acheron ate, he took in the lay of the land. He noticed the gravel driveway that had rounded the house led to a good sized garage or shop-like building. The backyard only stretched about twenty paces before hitting trees. He pointed at them.

"I smell water. How big's your stream?"

Rusty told him that the house was situated on a twenty-five acre parcel. The stream ran year round, although during the hot summer months it thinned quite a bit in places. There was one area he'd dug out a bit so his cat had a place to play in the water.

Acheron looked forward to checking it out.

Almost thirty minutes later, with dinner winding down, Korvyn told them, "So, I'm going to help carry everything into the house, and then I'm going to get out of your hair." He grinned at Rusty, and he gave his brother a suggestive smile. "Give you your privacy, so you can bond."

Rusty rubbed the back of his neck as he held Korvyn's gaze. "You really don't have to do that." He mumbled the words as his cheeks took on a pinkish hue.

"Sure I do, man." Korvyn's expression cleared, turning earnest. "You need time alone with your mate." He reached over and grabbed his brother's hand. "This is a big change for you. I get that. But a good one."

Korvyn released Rusty's hand and began stacking plates and silverware. As he worked, he glanced Acheron's way. "You be good to my brother, man, or I'll find a way to make you pay. Got it?"

Acheron nodded as heat suffused his body. "He is my everything now. His happiness brings me happiness."

"Good." Korvyn wheeled backward a couple feet, then placed the pile of dishes onto his lap. "I'll be home tomorrow before I head to work."

"Where are you going?" Rusty rose from his chair and picked up a couple of bowls, so Acheron did the same, grabbing the meat platter.

"I'm spending the night at the gang's rented lodge." Korvyn grinned and led the way into the house. "Gonna enjoy a little eye candy, and maybe I'll even see if any of those guys they rescued are interested in some fun."

"Thank you for being so considerate." Acheron placed the platter on the counter. "It is very thoughtful of you."

"Well, to be honest, it was Adam's idea." Korvyn turned his chair so he could grin at them both. "After he heard you were coming here for dinner, he gave me a ring. He told me about how intense it can be when two shifters come together for the first time." Waggling his brows, he added, "How... one-track-minded they can be in terms of getting their hands on—"

Rusty grabbed the back of Korvyn's chair in one hand and slapped his other over his brother's mouth. "Right." He scowled at his brother. "We get it."

When Rusty drew his hand away, Korvyn sat there beaming. The man obviously enjoyed getting underneath Rusty's skin. Maybe it was a brother thing.

"Well, Adam would know," Acheron commented, shaking his head. The white tiger shifter definitely had a big mouth. "And while I'd never purposefully try to run you out of your home, it's very kind of you to consider your brother's comfort in the matter."

Korvyn grinned up at Acheron as he leaned forward and patted his thigh. "You're pretty formal, Acheron. We're gonna have to work on that." Then he turned to Rusty. "I like him, though." Gliding toward the mudroom, he added, "I can get the rest of the stuff outside if you two wanna load it all into the dishwasher. Then I'll scram."

Acheron watched the man wheel out of the room, then turned his attention to Rusty. He saw how his mate's head was bowed and his cheeks were flushed. The man practically screamed discomfort.

Sliding his left hand along Rusty's chest as he eased by him, Acheron flicked his mate's nipple lightly. Gratification filled him when he heard the cat shifter's breath catch. He also noticed his gaze snap to Acheron's and how his nipples beaded.

Smiling at Rusty, Acheron offered, "Your brother is very considerate." After taking in Rusty's uncertain expression as he nodded, he got to work loading the dishwasher. Taking into account his mate's skittishness, he decided to give Rusty something else to focus on other than the heavy scents of arousal perfuming the air. "Do you have a particular way you like your dishwasher filled?"

That was a thing, right?

CHAPTER SEVEN

True to his word, Korvyn brought in the remaining dishes then headed to his room. He returned a few minutes later with an overnight bag. Stopping near the dining room table, he said his goodbyes.

Acheron responded with, "It was nice to meet you, and drive safely," as Rusty crossed to his brother.

Korvyn responded with a thumbs up, then focused on Rusty.

Placing his hand on Korvyn's shoulder, Rusty squeezed lightly. "Thanks for understanding, and—" He didn't know how to finish his sentence.

Resting his hand over Rusty's where it was on his shoulder, Korvyn murmured, "I'm real happy for you, Rusty. After everything you've done for the family, you deserve something just for you."

Rusty's heart warmed as his throat closed. He nodded, since he was unable to find his voice. Korvyn patted his hand, then placed them both on his wheels and headed toward the front door.

Shoving his hands into his pockets, Rusty crossed to the front window and stared outside vacantly. He started when he felt lean arms wrap around him from behind. Acheron rubbed his palms over his stomach and chest soothingly, and Rusty relaxed in his hold.

"You worry about him?" Acheron murmured as he rested his cheek against Rusty's back between his shoulder blades.

Rusty nodded, settling his hands over Acheron's, rubbing

lightly. "He puts on a good façade, but some days are hard for him."

"But he has you and now me." Acheron squeezed his torso, then relaxed his arms again. "Did you trick out a vehicle for him?"

Hearing the rumble of a vehicle's engine, Rusty nodded. "Yeah. A small van. One of the reasons I became a mechanic," he revealed softly. Scoffing, he added, "Never admitted that to anyone before."

Acheron hummed, then pressed a dry kiss to the back of Rusty's neck. "And his comment about all you've done for your family?"

Rusty hesitated, but knew he needed to share with his mate at some point. "Well, when my mother and brother were in that accident, mother fought a bout of depression." Sifting through his memories of that time, he explained, "Father was already on the outs with the pride, since he went against his alpha and chose to bond with a human." Peering over his shoulder, he caught Acheron's gaze. "The alpha at the time was kind of an asshole."

Acheron gave him a wry smile. "Sadly, there are a number of them out there."

Agreeing wholeheartedly, Rusty nodded. "My father went to part-time, so he could stay home with mother and Korvyn. Since he was no longer contributing much to the pride, they cut him off, so I got a part-time job after school at a mechanic shop to help pay bills." He shrugged. "I discovered I have a knack for it, and I find it interesting, so I'm certainly not sorry about falling into that line of work."

"And you've been doing it ever since."

Rusty nodded upon hearing Acheron's words.

"You are an amazing man," Acheron crooned. "Taking care of your family that way."

While Rusty appreciated Acheron's words, he didn't

really feel that way. "It's what had to be done." He whispered the words as he watched Korvyn's van slowly trundle down the driveway, then turn left onto the road, and disappear in the distance.

Listening to Acheron hum thoughtfully, Rusty turned in his mate's grip. He wrapped his arms around the smaller man and dipped his head, burying his face against Acheron's neck. Inhaling deeply, Rusty enjoyed his mate's scent.

"Smell so good," Rusty mumbled. "I'm sorry I walked away from you yesterday. I was..." His voice trailed off as he struggled to come up with the right word.

Acheron rubbed up and down his back, tracing the knobs of his spine. He pressed a kiss to Rusty's neck as he softly responded, "Shocked, uncertain, overwhelmed?"

Rusty snickered as he rubbed his shaved cheek along the smooth skin of Acheron's neck. "I was going to go with an asshole, but overwhelmed definitely works." He slipped out his tongue and swiped it along Acheron's skin, relishing the light salty flavor of his mate. "You're right," he whispered. "I do jump to conclusions, especially when it's about anything to do with relationships that could disrupt my family." Lifting his head, Rusty peered into Acheron's dark eyes. "Can you forgive me?"

"There's nothing to forgive, Rusty," Acheron stated quietly, his near-black-eyed gaze serene. "We are here now. We are mates. We will work it out."

Acheron's smile filled with heat as he skimmed one hand down, slipping it beneath Rusty's polo shirt so he could finger along the waistband of Rusty's jeans. He slid his other hand up, then over Rusty's upper arm, to finally land on his shoulder. Acheron teased at the skin where his neck met his shoulder, right where Rusty knew he'd give him a claiming bite.

"What we need to decide now is... how quickly are we going to give in to our need to bond?"

A groan ripped from Rusty's throat as tingles worked through him. They started at the dual points where Acheron's fingertips teased, causing his nipples to tighten and bead as well as blood to flood his groin. His head swam as he gave himself over to the delicious sensations, and he tipped his head back in pleasure.

"Oh, you do look amazing when flooded with need," Acheron stated, a growl in his voice. He cradled Rusty's neck and tugged at the hairs on his nape. "But I need words, my mate. I won't jump to conclusions again." Leaning up, Acheron pressed a kiss to the bottom of his chin, then scraped his teeth along his jawline. "Talk to me," he insisted. "Tell me what you want."

"You," Rusty blurted out, finally finding his tongue. "You, my mate." When he inhaled deeply, his senses sang with the exquisite smells of their combined arousal. Rusty dipped his chin down, rubbing his cheek along Acheron's face, and finally met his mate's gaze. "You're mine, and I'm yours, and I want us to build a life together."

Acheron's dark eyes sparkled, and a pleased smile curved his lips. "Me, too." He glanced over his shoulder toward the hall. "Will you show me to your room?"

Anticipation warred with a spike of nerves, but still Rusty nodded. "Yeah." He was under no illusion about who was dominant in the relationship. His cat longed to submit to his mate.

"Now, then?" Acheron urged. Nibbling along his jawbone, he added, "Or would you prefer to curl up on the sofa and talk some more?"

"Don't wanna sit and talk." Rusty groaned softly before he managed to admit, "I'd already be leading you to my room, but I don't seem to be able to pull away from you."

Acheron rumbled a deep husky chuckle. "Hmm, then I'd

best let you go."

While Rusty nodded in reply, he still moaned roughly when Acheron eased away from him.

Laughing again, Acheron slid his hands down Rusty's forearm, then gripped his hand. "Lead the way," he ordered, squeezing his fingers.

Rusty pulled himself together and did as his mate urged. He led the way across the living room and down the hall.

The home was a three bedroom ranch with two bathrooms. They'd turned the first, smallest bedroom into a home gym, allowing Korvyn to keep his body in shape as much as possible. His brother also had the larger, master bedroom, since he needed the space to easily maneuver his chair. They'd also remodeled the master bathroom to accommodate his needs.

Opening his own bedroom's door, Rusty took a second to point at a closed door across the hall. "That's my bathroom, should you need it."

Acheron grinned, nodding. "Not yet." He waggled his brows. "But good to know so I can clean you up after blowing your mind."

Upon hearing the husky note of promise in Acheron's tone, Rusty felt a shudder work through his body. His hard cock twitched behind his fly. He even imagined he could feel the pre-cum leak from him.

Inhaling sharply, Acheron growled low in his throat. He rested his hand on Rusty's lower back and pushed gently. Rusty obeyed the silent order and entered his room, crossing to the bed. He felt Acheron's heat, telling him he stayed oh-so-close behind him.

"Last chance to change your mind," Acheron rumbled into his ear as he slid his palm up his back. His second hand joined his first, massaging over his shoulder blades and coming to rest on his shoulders. He tipped closer to whisper, "If we climb into that bed, I will claim you, Rusty."

Feeling his heart trip in his chest, Rusty trembled. He gathered his courage and turned, taking in the hungry expression on Acheron's face. His feline rowled in the back of his mind, urging him on.

Rusty agreed with his cat. He loved the fact that he was the cause of Acheron's need. Letting out a possessive growl of his own, he wrapped his arms around his mate and pulled him close.

"You're mine, too," Rusty declared. "My mate. No other will touch you." Remembering Acheron's admittance of how much he liked sex, he declared, "You will get all you need from *me.*"

Acheron rubbed up his chest as he pressed against Rusty's body. He gave Rusty a feral grin. "That's right, my sexy cat. Exactly right."

Rusty held Acheron's heated gaze for several seconds, reading his soon-to-be lover's possessive intent. The promise filling his eyes nearly took Rusty's breath away.

Breaking the stare-down, Acheron lifted onto his toes and pressed a light kiss to Rusty's lips. "Can't wait to see all of you, touch all of you," he murmured, drawing back a little. At the same time, he scraped his fingernails lightly down Rusty's chest and gripped his shirt. "Arms up."

Goose bumps broke out on Rusty's arms, and his nipples beaded. He obeyed, raising his arms. When Acheron lifted his shirt, he bent at the waist, making it easy for his shorter mate to pull his shirt from him.

When Rusty opened his eyes and straightened, his mouth went dry. The appreciative gaze that Acheron swept over his torso caused his lungs to seize. After dropping Rusty's shirt to the floor, Acheron boldly reached up and pinched his nipples.

Rusty moaned roughly, and he trembled.

Acheron grinned, his dark eyes hot. He rubbed his hands down Rusty's lean torso, tracing over his abdominals, then teased into the waistband of his cargo shorts. He scraped along the grooves of his V, causing his cock to jerk behind his fly.

Humming, Acheron focused on his groin as he continued to tease the sensitive flesh under his waistband. "Now, let's see the beautiful cock I can't wait to taste."

Parting his lips, Rusty panted softly. He stared down, watching with anticipation as Acheron popped the button on his fly. His breath shuddered in his chest as his mate began working down the zipper one slow tooth at a time.

Rusty moaned as fiery tendrils of need caused his stomach muscles to twitch. His oozing prick was slowly revealed, his hard length pressing from between the flaps. Acheron wasted no time in teasing his fingertips up and down his length, causing the skin of his groin to goose bump and his balls to tingle.

Never had someone teased him in such a manner, and delicious, tingly shivers racked his body. His head tipped back, and his eyelids slid shut. His fingers twitched at his sides as he reveled in the sensations his mate created with such simple touches.

"Step out of your shorts, Rusty, and climb onto the bed."

Snapping back to himself, Rusty blinked. He managed to focus on Acheron, who was peering at him with an expression on his face that was equal parts smug and feral. It took a few deep breaths, but Rusty managed to get himself moving.

CHAPTER EIGHT

Gods, Rusty responds better than any dream. Magnificent.
Acheron watched Rusty turn and begin climbing on the bed, his globes flexing and his hole winking at him provocatively. "So damn pretty." Acheron swiftly yanked off his own shirt before he could get caught up in the gorgeous view.

Once Acheron had stripped, he returned his focus to Rusty. His mate had flipped to his back and was staring at him with a mixture of need and nerves. Acheron noticed his prick had softened a little, too.

I can fix that.

"Relax," Acheron crooned as he levered onto the bed. As he crawled toward him, he raked his gaze over Rusty's lean lines. "I will make your body soar."

Rusty nodded even as he nibbled his bottom lip.

Acheron paused for an instant. "Shit," he mumbled, drawing away.

"What is it?"

Not liking the trepidation filling Rusty's voice, Acheron quickly assured, "Nothing. Just almost forgot one of the most important bits." He leaned over the side of the bed and grabbed his pants. An instant later, he rose back to his knees, dropping the pants. Holding Rusty's gaze, Acheron winked and grinned as he held up his prize. "Lube."

Nodding again, Rusty offered a tentative smile. "Shoulda told you it was in the nightstand."

"I didn't want to presume," Acheron told his lover as he

knee-walked toward his soon-to-be lover.

To Acheron's surprise, Rusty grinned up at him. "And bringing your own lube isn't presuming?"

Laughing lightly, Acheron shrugged before levering over Rusty, resting his weight on his left hand. "More a matter of wishful thinking," he admitted, then lowered his body and sprawled over his mate.

Acheron grunted at the first sweet pressure of his cock against his mate's. Gently grinding his erection against Rusty's own, he enjoyed the way his cat shifter's lips parted and a soft gasp escaped him. Rusty's eyes dilated, and he rested his hands on Acheron's hips, clutching at him.

Resting his weight on the elbow of his left arm, that hand still clutching the lube, Acheron slid his right fingers up into Rusty's hair. He scratched at his scalp lightly as he urged his mate to dip his head. As soon as Rusty obeyed the pressure, Acheron brushed his lips over his mate's in a light, teasing caress.

Rusty slid his hands up Acheron's back, his grip tightening. Acheron worked soft kisses along his jaw, then down his neck. He smiled as he did so, liking how Rusty tipped his chin up, giving him plenty of room to work.

Moving down Rusty's neck, Acheron kissed and licked along the tendon. He enjoyed the light, salty flavor of his mate's skin as he eased along his torso. When he scraped his teeth over one swollen bud, Rusty shook beneath him. Acheron took a few seconds to work his man's nipple with his lips. He released Rusty's hair, so he could use that hand to pinch and roll his other nub.

Rusty groaned and whimpered. Rubbing his hands over Acheron's shortly cropped head, he arched into his touch and cried out his name. He then rocked his hips up, sliding his prick over Acheron's stomach, clearly searching for friction.

Happy to give it to him, since that would help move things along, Acheron mouthed his way down Rusty's stomach. For an instant, he peered through his lashes up his mate's body, taking in his flushed, sweat-dampened flesh as well as the expression of ecstasy etched on his features. Then he opened his mouth and swallowed Rusty's cock to the root.

Rusty cried out his name and bucked, nearly knocking Acheron sideways. He eased up and off his prick, earning him a cry of dismay from his mate. "Easy," he crooned, mouthing kisses along his shaft. "Breathe for me, sexy cat."

While Acheron whispered assurances and teased Rusty's cock and balls with his lips, teeth, and tongue, he opened the lube and poured a generous dollop onto his fingers. He caressed his mate's stomach soothingly, tracing over his balls with his thumb as he slid his fingertips between his legs. When Acheron brushed his slicked digits over Rusty's hole, he opened his mouth and wrapped his lips around his crown.

Acheron pushed, sinking his middle finger in deep. Calling on years of experience, he nailed his mate's prostate on the first try.

Rusty made a noise that sounded like a cross between a gasp and a hiccup. "A-Ach!" he cried, jerking in his grip.

Humming, Acheron eased his finger partway out, then pushed in all the way. At the same time, he eased farther down on Rusty's dick. By the time he was sucking up on his erection once more, he had sunk his digit in as deeply as possible again.

"A-Ach! Acheron. Oh!" Rusty babbled as he began to rock his hips. "Th-That's — what — ugh!"

Acheron peered up Rusty's body as he worked his lean shifter. The look of ecstasy on his cat shifter's face was a thing of beauty, and Acheron knew he'd want to see it over and over again. When Rusty moved his hands off of Acheron's head and gripped the comforter, then began to rock his hips, he didn't try to stay his movements.

Instead, Acheron took advantage.

Allowing Rusty to fuck his mouth, then push back onto his fingers, Acheron eased a second digit into his chute. His lover only paused in his movements for a second, then he resumed his rutting. Acheron continued to peg Rusty's prostate every few jerks while sucking strongly on his mate's prick. Swiping his tongue over the other shifter's swollen crown, he cleared away the pre-cum and swallowed the lightly salted goodness down.

Rusty suddenly gasped and tensed. His hips jolted under his ministrations. That was the only warning Acheron received before his mouth was filled with Rusty's cream.

Acheron pushed a third finger into Rusty's channel as he eased partway off his cock. He continued to suck and swallow on his prick. Gently petting his shuddering lover's twitching abdominals, he did his best to heighten his release.

At the same time, Acheron finished stretching him.

When Rusty finally stopped spurting, Acheron eased off his dick. It pleased him that his lover's cock remained mostly hard. Sliding his fingertips down his stomach, then through Rusty's spit-dampened pubes, he tugged them lightly. He teased his fingertips up the underside of his mate's prick, distracting him as he pulled his fingers free of his channel.

Gripping his own erection, Acheron coated himself with the remaining slick. He moved forward, levering over his lover. Peering down, he swept his gaze over Rusty's torso, taking in his deeply flushed chest, beaded nipples, and heavy-lidded, relaxed expression.

"So gorgeous, my mate," Acheron murmured, holding his gaze. "Now, I will make you mine."

Rusty nodded, his eyes seeming to glow. "Yes, please.

Yours."

"All mine."

Excitement of a different sort skittered through Acheron. After so many years of searching, he had found his one and only, his mate, his home.

Acheron gripped the base of his dick and pressed the crown to Rusty's stretched hole. "Breathe deeply, love," he urged as he applied light pressure. "And push out."

For a split second, it felt as if Rusty resisted, then he let out a long breath. Acheron felt his body relax. He rocked his hips forward and, holding his mate's gaze, felt his crown ease inside his man.

Rusty's eyes widened, and his jaw sagged open. He hissed softly and tensed.

Needing Rusty to remain relaxed, Acheron fisted the fingers covered in lube and rested his weight on that arm's forearm. He pressed close to his lover and nibbled on his collarbone. At the same time, he used his clean hand to tease at one of Rusty's nipples.

"Breathe," Acheron encouraged again, continuing his ministrations. His body practically vibrated with his need to move, to sink deeper. "Here is where I'm going to bite you, Rusty." Acheron scraped his teeth over the tendon in Rusty's neck. "I will sink my teeth in deep and drink your blood, sealing our mating. You'll be mine, and I'll be yours."

When Acheron sucked on the tendon again, Rusty moaned and tipped his head to the side, offering more room. His arms came around Acheron's torso, gripping at his shoulder blades. Rusty began to move restlessly beneath him.

Acheron also noticed the clench on his cock head easing.

Taking that as the cue it was, while continuing his teasing onslaught on Rusty's body, Acheron started to move. He pushed in a little, then eased partway out again. With each rut, he pushed deeper and deeper into his lover.

Groaning at the exquisite sensation, the tight grip encasing more and more of his cock, Acheron felt his canines tingle. He didn't even try stopping them from lengthening as his anticipation to bite flooded him. His nostrils flared as he scented Rusty's once again rising arousal.

"That's it." Acheron would forever deny any whine in his voice. "Enjoy my taking."

"Hell, yeah." Groaning deeply, Rusty rocked into Acheron's movements. "Right there. So good!"

Realizing he was pressing against Rusty's prostate with each gliding pass, Acheron made sure to stay at that angle as he sped up his thrusts. He slid his hand up his lover's torso to his neck, then slid his fingers into his hair. Tightening his hold, he used it to tip his mate's head down.

Acheron leaned up a little, never allowing his hips to slow. He took in Rusty's heavy-lidded expression and how he panted between slightly parted lips. Every couple of thrusts, a whimper, hiss, or moan escaped Rusty.

Never had Acheron seen such a gorgeous sight. His cock throbbed in response, and his balls began to tingle. Wanting Rusty to come with him, to offer his mate waves of bliss, Acheron released his lover's hair and reached between them.

To Acheron's pleasure, he discovered Rusty's cock hard and leaking. He gripped his mate's length and stroked him in time with his ruts. At the same time, he lowered his head back to Rusty's neck and scraped his sharp canines along his tendon.

"Come for me," Acheron crooned, speeding up his ministrations. "I want to feel you squeeze me, my mate." He nipped lightly at Rusty's shoulder, then nibbled up his neck. "Milk my cock."

"Yesss," Rusty hissed. "So good. Oh! Love your hand on my dick. Faster."

Doing as Rusty requested, Acheron worked his mate. The man's groans stopped to be replaced by babbles and nonsensical mumblings. Between that and the sounds of flesh slapping against flesh and the thick smell of arousal perfuming the air, Acheron didn't know how he would manage to hang on.

To Acheron's relief, Rusty's body seized beneath him. His cock jerked in his hold. The muscles of the chute encasing his length rippled in pulsing squeezes.

Enjoying the best kind of massage, Acheron relished the feel of Rusty's seed coating their stomachs. The heady scent of his mate's cum filled his nostrils. The base of Acheron's spine tingled, and his balls pulled tight.

Acheron's orgasm swelled through him, flooding his body with ecstasy. It crashed through him in mind-numbing waves. He groaned with bliss as he slowed his ruts, filling Rusty's body with his release.

Unable to wait an instant longer, Acheron sank his teeth into Rusty's flesh, claiming what was his. Rusty jolted in his arms, so he released his mate's prick and gripped his shoulder, holding him steady. Sucking on the wound, Acheron drew more of his mate's exquisite life fluid into his mouth.

Rusty let out a throaty groan and shuddered in Acheron's hold. As Acheron pulled more blood from his bite, he hummed, appreciating the influx of the aroma of Rusty's cum, telling him his mate had come again. After one more satisfying mouthful of Rusty's blood, Acheron eased his teeth from his mate's flesh. He lapped over his mark, overwhelmed by the pride he felt at seeing it on his mate.

Sliding his focus to Rusty's face, Acheron took in his lover's sated expression as well as the relaxed smile curving his lips.

"Absolutely stunning," Acheron whispered, meeting his mate's gaze. "And all mine."

CHAPTER NINE

Rusty panted, trying to catch his breath. His body felt lethargic, sweaty, and sated. He couldn't remember the last time he'd felt so good and so exhausted all at the same time.

Meeting Acheron's gaze, Rusty took in his lover's relaxed contented smile. His expression held a wealth of satisfaction and... not love, exactly, but definite warmth. Rusty's heart skipped a beat at the sight.

When Rusty processed Acheron's words, he hummed. "Yeah. Yours." Rubbing his hands up and down his mate's back, he murmured, "Just as you are mine."

Acheron nodded. "Hell, yeah."

Rusty swept his gaze over Acheron's dark, sweaty skin. Running his palms up Acheron's lean back, then over his shoulders, Rusty admired the differences between them. He really liked how his lighter skin contrasted with his mate's.

"Just relax there," Acheron urged, his voice soft and husky. "I'm going to get something to clean us up."

Rusty nodded, and Acheron dipped his head. He pressed his lips to Rusty's and teased them with his tongue. Rusty immediately opened, and Acheron slipped the warm muscle into his mouth, mapping him in slow, languorous strokes.

At the same time, Acheron eased his softened dick out of Rusty's passage. Rusty fed his mate a grunt at the unfamiliar sensation. His chute felt oddly stretched and weirdly empty.

As strange as being taken had felt, Rusty couldn't wait to be filled by his mate again.

Acheron eased the kiss to an end, nipping Rusty's bottom lip lightly in the process. He grinned down at him. "Be right back."

Rusty returned the man's smile, then watched in silence as the lean shifter eased off the bed. Watching Acheron stride across the room and exit through the doorway, he found his gaze riveted to his lover's ass. The dark brown globes were high and tight, not quite a bubble butt, but close.

His fingers twitched with a desire to touch.

Once Acheron was out of sight, Rusty closed his eyes and heaved a deep sigh. He relaxed on the comforter beneath him. Hearing the faucet run in the bathroom, an image popped into his head—his mate in the shower, water trickling in enticing rivulets down his lean naked form. Since it wasn't the shower running, Rusty's thoughts swiftly changed to Acheron provocatively rubbing a damp cloth over his chest and groin.

Noticing a slight tickle between his ass cheeks pulled Rusty from his imaginings. He winced when he realized the cause.

Rolling over, Rusty reached over to the nightstand and pulled several tissues from the box on it. He ignored the stickiness on his chest in favor of wiping between his thighs. Making a mental note to toss the comforter in the washing machine, Rusty threw the soiled tissues into the garbage by the bed.

"I'd intended to do that," Acheron said, revealing he'd returned.

Rusty turned his attention to his mate, watching him cross to the bed with a cloth in each hand—one wet, one dry. His lover's expression appeared concerned. Stopping beside the bed, Acheron placed the dry towel near his hip, then began wiping down his groin.

His cheeks ignited, and Rusty shuttered his gaze. He didn't stop Acheron's actions. Still, being cleaned by another, even his lover, somehow felt so much more intimate than the act they'd just shared.

Clearing his throat, Rusty mumbled, "Sorry. It felt odd." He flicked his gaze to Acheron's face, then glanced around the room. "And, well, new experience and all."

"Sorry I wasn't quicker," Acheron responded. His lover's deep voice was a melodious rumble and drew Rusty's focus to his face. Offering a lascivious smile, Acheron told him, "Don't worry, though. You'll grow used to the occasional mess." He waggled his brows before finishing, "Other times, we'll keep it clean... like in the bathroom at your work when we enjoy a nooner."

Rusty gaped for an instant, then barked a laugh. Relaxing, he rolled his eyes. "So very sure of yourself, are you?"

Acheron began rubbing the cloth over his groin, then up his stomach and torso. He hummed softly. "With you, always, my sexy kitty."

Feeling his skin heat and his blood warm just from Acheron's cleaning ministrations, Rusty shivered. "Yeah." His voice came out breathier than he could ever remember sounding, but having his naked, sexy mate leaning over him and touching him so intimately was doing funny things to him. "Gods, if you don't stop that"—Rusty realized that Acheron had finished cleaning and was now tracing his pectorals and teasing his nipples—"I'm going to get hard again."

Acheron offered him a hungry smile. "Is that such a bad thing?"

Remembering his mate's admission about loving sex, Rusty sucked in a harsh breath. His nostrils flared, and he shook his head. Deciding to do a little touching of his own, Rusty rocked up. He grabbed his mate and twisted, sending him sprawling, this time with Rusty half on top of him.

Laughing, the sound one of joy and pleasure, Acheron grinned up at him as he threaded his fingers through Rusty's hair. He lightly scratched at his scalp, and Rusty purred softly. He hadn't even been aware he could make the sound while in human form, but damn was his mate's touch amazing.

Obviously, Acheron had figured out how much Rusty liked it, too. He used his hold to urge Acheron closer. Before their lips touched, the trill of a phone interrupted them.

Rusty froze, not recognizing the ringtone. He lifted a brow in silent question. Acheron's brows furrowed, his eyes telling of his confusion.

"I have no idea who'd call me. Kontra's people gave me that phone, since I'd originally planned to travel with them for a while."

"And they all know you're here getting to know your mate." Rusty levered off Acheron, and his mate groaned, his annoyance clear. Easing to a sitting position, Rusty added, "They wouldn't have called if it wasn't important."

Acheron rolled and crawled to the edge of the bed. "Yeah." Leaning down, he grabbed his jeans.

As Acheron fished his phone out of his pocket, Rusty took advantage of the position and skimmed his fingertips down his lover's butt cheek.

Growling softly, Acheron glanced over at him as he straightened, but his expression was playful. "Yeah?" he asked, pressing the phone to his ear.

"Hey, Ach. I'm real sorry to interrupt. Just got a quick question."

Rusty recognized Adam's voice, his shifter hearing making it easy to make out the words.

"Sure, man." Acheron leered at Rusty. "But make it quick. I'm a little preoccupied."

"Uh... oookay." Adam sounded confused. "I'm calling about Korvyn. We'd offered him a place here for a day or two while you and Rusty got acquainted. Did he decide to stay there and, uh—"

"Wait. What?" Rusty grabbed the phone from Acheron. "Korvyn left"—he glanced at the clock on the nightstand—"over an hour ago. He should have been there by now."

"Would he have stopped anywhere first? Maybe at a friend's or he decided to go to a fuck buddy's, instead?" Adam hesitated an instant, then added, "Because I tried his phone, and he's not answering."

Rusty swallowed hard, his pulse spiking. "N-No." He whispered the one word.

"You sure, Rusty?" Adam prodded.

Opening his mouth, Rusty snapped it closed again. He didn't know what to say.

Acheron reached out and gently tugged the phone from his grip. With his other hand, he threaded their fingers together. Into the phone, he stated, "Even if he'd stopped for gas, he would have made it to you by now. He mentioned seeing if any of the new humans still under Kontra's care would be interested in a little fun, so stopping at a fuck buddy's place is definitely out."

Rusty rubbed his free hand over his face, struggling to get his mind to engage. Rising from the bed, he pulled away from Acheron, who gave him a questioning look. Rusty grabbed his pants from the floor and began pulling them on.

"Tell Adam I'm going to retrace Korvyn's steps. I need to be certain he hasn't been in an accident. I—"

Rusty heard his phone chime, cutting him off midstream. Turning, he searched for his phone, locating it on his dresser. Crossing to it, he snagged it and read the screen.

A deep sigh of relief filled him as he answered. "Hey, Korvyn. Adam just called. We were worried about you."

"You should be worried."

Rusty didn't recognize the voice. "Who are you? Where's Korvyn?" A shiver of fear worked through him, the sensation there and gone, eased by Acheron crossing to his side and rubbing his back soothingly.

"Let's just say... I'm someone who you shouldn't steal from," the smooth-sounding voice replied. "And Korvyn is here with me. Currently he's fine, but he won't stay that way if you and your friends don't return my property to me."

Acheron growled softly. "He's the fucking buyer." He hissed the words just loud enough to reach Rusty's ear.

"The buyer?" Rusty repeated softly.

It must have been loud enough, for the man chuckled, the sound cruel. "Good. You know of me."

Rusty curled his lip in a sneer. "What do you want?"

"I told you. My property," the man replied. "I paid for eight pieces of merchandise, and I mean to have them. Forty miles north of town is the trailhead for the Kerns hiking trail. Have your friends drop them off there by midnight."

"Or what?" The words were out of Rusty's mouth before he could think better of them.

The chuckle that sounded through the line was low and cruel. "Do you really need me to spell it out for you, foolish man? Do you want to hear how I'll return your brother to you piece by piece until I get what I want?"

Rusty growled, anger replacing his fear and concern. "You're an animal," he claimed harshly. "Dealing in human flesh... I don't know where all the *men* are that you're trying to steal the lives of."

"But your friends know," the man countered. "You have just over four hours. Better hurry."

"Wait!" Rusty cried. "Where's Korvyn? I want to talk to him. Prove to me that he's still alive."

The silence lasted so long that Rusty actually checked to

make certain the connection was still open. Finally, he heard Korvyn's voice, and relief rushed through him.

"Rusty, don't do it," Korvyn told him. "We don't trade in lives."

"Oh, Korvyn," Rusty murmured, bowing his head. He sagged into Acheron's embrace, certain he would have hit the floor if his mate hadn't been there to hold him up. "I'm so sorry."

"None of this is your fault. I—"

"I've done as you requested," the leader stated. "Now, drop off my merchandise where I ordered. I won't be there and neither will Korvyn, but I'll know if it's been done." His voice lowered, taking on an edge of warning. "And if it hasn't been... well... Korvyn thought his life was hard before."

"You son of a bitch," Rusty snarled.

The man began to laugh, the sound cutting Rusty to the bone before the line went dead.

"I'm so fucking sorry," Acheron whispered, holding Rusty close. Rusty peered at his mate in confusion, and Acheron answered his unspoken question. "If I hadn't barged into your life until after Kontra had found this guy, Korvyn would still be here and safe. I—"

"Stop it," Rusty snapped, glaring at the smaller man. "This is not your fault, and we're going to bloody well fix this."

Vindictive rage surged through Rusty's veins as he straightened his spine. He cradled Acheron's jaw between both palms and peered into his eyes. Seeing the fear and concern in his mate's eyes, Rusty realized from where it stemmed.

My mate fears I'll blame him.

"This is *not* your fault," Rusty repeated before dipping his head and pressing a kiss to Acheron's lips. Lifting his head, he held his gaze. "We'll call Kontra on the way to their place.

I know he and his people will be able to come up with a plan."

"They already know. Adam was still on my phone's line, and he heard everything."

"Good." Rubbing a soothing hand over Acheron's naked torso, he enjoyed the feel of his smooth skin. Still, he knew he couldn't get distracted, so after pecking one more kiss to Acheron's lips, he eased away as he urged, "Get dressed, so we can ride."

Acheron's eyes narrowed, and his expression turned almost feral. "Then after we deal with this asshole once and for all, we'll bring Korvyn home and pick up right where we left off."

Rusty nodded.

Gripping Rusty's nape, Acheron pulled his head down. He captured his mouth in a deep, tongue-fucking, toe-curling kiss, mapping him swiftly. A few seconds later, Acheron broke the kiss and stepped back. He swatted Rusty's ass, ordering, "Hurry up."

His heart feeling lighter than he had any right to feel knowing Korvyn was in danger, Rusty obeyed. His dominant lover was back, and somehow, they'd figure out how to bring his brother home.

CHAPTER TEN

A cheron knew that Rusty didn't like the plan. Neither did a couple of other shifters, since their mates were being placed in harms' way, too. Still, Acheron had confidence that it would work.

Of the eight original twinks that had been kidnapped and rescued, only four were part of the group being left at the trailhead. It was Deter, Louis, Elron, and himself. The other twinks were made up of Caleb, a chameleon shifter, Sam, a wolf shifter, and Yuma, a penguin shifter. The fourth man was Kontra's own mate, Tim, who was a warlock.

While all the men were on the smaller side, the fact that most of them were shifters gave them increased strength, speed, and agility. Not to mention Tim had magick, and Elron — being a fae — had talents of his own.

The mates of everyone drove, except for Louis, who was being driven by Adam.

"Everything will be fine," Acheron assured Rusty. Sitting behind him on his Goldwing, he rubbed his hands up and down his sides, trying to soothe him. "Kontra's people are in place, hiding in the trees and shit, waiting to capture the people that come to pick us up."

Over half a dozen of Kontra's people had already left the gang's rented cabin even before Acheron and Rusty had managed to arrive. That group was led by Beta Sam and included a second warlock who was also a vampire — Draven.

"I still don't like the idea of leaving my mate to be picked up by a group of human traffickers," Rusty grumbled.

"None of us do." Kontra's voice sounded through the microphone's helmet. "But this is the easiest way to find out where Korvyn is being held."

"The guy said he wouldn't be there and neither would Korvyn," Rusty pointed out. "How does it help us?"

"Draven isn't just a warlock," Adam explained. "He's a vampire. We need to capture all these assholes alive, and he can do some freaky mind control shit and make one of them tell us all about his boss's operation, where he's hiding, and what kind of force he has protecting them." The big, white tiger shifter chuckled coldly. "Then we go wipe them out."

The group again fell into silence.

Acheron prayed to whatever god that cared to listen that it would be that easy.

They pulled into the driveway, and the eight motorcycles rolled to a stop in the parking area. As soon as Acheron dismounted, Rusty followed suit. His lover wrapped his arms around him and pressed a kiss to his lips. Dipping his head, he nuzzled Acheron's temple, whispering, "We'll be together soon."

"Yes, we will." Acheron believed that with all his heart.

"If you get injured, I'm going to kick your ass," Rusty told him roughly.

Acheron chuckled as he peered into Rusty's amber-eyed gaze. "You could try, love." He pecked another kiss to Rusty's lips as he rubbed his palms up and down his sides underneath his leather jacket. He wished he could have felt his mate's skin rather than the fabric of his flannel shirt. "Be ready to go rescue your brother. Got it?"

Rusty nodded.

"Are the circles ready?"

Kontra's question drew Acheron's attention. He watched as the big bear shifter's mate nodded. "Yeah. We're all set up."

Glancing around, Acheron had no clue where said circles were. He did, however, know that they were referring to something magickal. He didn't bother trying to figure it out. Before meeting up with Kontra and his gang, he'd never had anything to do with a magick wielder and wasn't too worried about learning more.

Acheron heard Kontra order everyone, "Mount up."

Turning to his lover, Acheron watched Rusty obey. He stepped close and offered one more swift kiss, then he backed away. Joining the other seven men near a picnic table to the left of the trailhead information board, he sat on the grass. He preferred to be low to the ground if things went sideways.

"So, how long do you think we'll have to wait?" Louis asked, his arms wrapped around himself.

Yuma held the man, shrugging. "If they're watching, probably not long."

"Good," Caleb said on a growl. "I can't wait for them to get what's coming to them."

Sam nodded curtly, his brown lips curved into a feral smile.

"Don't worry, boys." Elron ran a slender-fingered hand through his long white hair as he smirked at them. "I'm sure they won't give their prizes time to run away."

As if on cue, as soon as the roar of the motorcycles had faded in the distance, footfalls crunching on leaves filled the air. Acheron lounged on his back as he turned his head. His excellent night vision helped him easily make out their guests.

"Wow, twelve men to take out us eight little twinks," Acheron jeered, sneering at the guy in the lead—a tall, wiry redhead. "Gotta say, that doesn't make us think much of you. Especially seein' as ya got guns and all."

Acheron knew by speaking, it drew the ringleader's attention to himself, and that was okay. Slowly, he rose to his feet and put himself in front of the others, crossing his arms over his chest. He stared defiantly at them.

"All of you, stand up and turn around," the redhead ordered, leveling his gun at Acheron's chest.

Even as Acheron heard some shuffling behind him—he also heard whispered chanting—he barked a laugh, covering the noise. "Oh, come off it, dude. We know you won't shoot us. We're the *merchandise.*" He lifted his fingers into air quotes as he glared at the man. "We're too valuable to damage like that."

The redhead glared at him. At the same time, seven other men holstered their side arms and closed the distance between them. The four other men spread out and kept their weapons trained on them.

"We might not get to shoot you," the redhead said, confirming Acheron's guess as he stalked toward him. His dark eyes glittered in the moonlight. After holstering his weapon, he cracked his knuckles. "But that don't mean we can't leave a few marks... as long as they're not on your pretty little faces."

Several of the other advancing men snickered.

Acheron lifted his hands, fisting them, as if ready to box the man. "Except now you're not facing a bunch of pliant, drugged men."

The redhead laughed again as he swept his gaze over him. "What a joke!"

"Naw," Acheron responded as he glanced around, seeing the position of the other men. He returned his focus to the would-be captor and winked. "I'm the distraction."

Tim followed that up by clapping his hands together and barking a word Acheron didn't recognize. Roaring flames burst up from the ground in two ovals. One surrounded the group of mates plus the redhead and one of the closer guards. The second one spread out wider, hopefully catching the rest of the men within its flaming walls.

"What the fuck?" the redhead cried.

Acheron laughed. "Yeah, you fucked with the wrong group this time." He sneered and waggled his brows. "How about you tell me where your boss is, where Korvyn is, and we'll think about going easy on ya?"

"I don't know how you're doing this, but stop it right now!" the second trapped guard cried, drawing his weapon.

Sam yanked off his t-shirt, shoved off his sweats, and began to shift. At the same time, both Caleb and Elron lunged toward the man. Yuma shoved Louis and Deter underneath the table.

Acheron leaped forward, grabbing the redhead's wrist before he could draw his weapon. The human tried to wrench away, so he jumped and used the momentum to swing around the man. Acheron wrapped his arms around the man's neck and initiated his shift.

As a small animal, Acheron didn't ever have to worry about shifting while clothed. He could easily crawl out of just about anything. Acheron also shifted damn fast.

After several heartbeats, the redhead began to look around, obviously trying to figure out where Acheron had gone. He must have noticed how the other guard was on his back. Sam's black wolf crouched and snarled over him, appearing almost feral in the firelight.

"Okay. Someone tell me what's going on," the redhead demanded. "Ernie! Where are you? Ted?"

Acheron realized he was calling to his men. Deciding it was time for lights out, Acheron sank his stinger into the redhead's neck. The redhead cried out and tried to slap at him. Skittering sideways, Acheron easily gripped the man's shirt and moved to the other side of his neck, then stung him again.

"Ow, fuck!" The redhead staggered, crying, "What?" then dropped.

Crawling away from the downed human, Acheron assessed the situation. He knew with a man that size and from two stings, he'd be out for a good hour. Acheron climbed up the table leg, spotting the humans under the table. Yuma stood beside Tim, who sat cross-legged on top of the table doing... something.

Yuma eyed him. "Acheron?"

Acheron couldn't very well answer or nod in his current form, so he clicked his pinchers. Then he pivoted, trying to make out movement beyond the ring of fire.

To Acheron's relief, he heard the howl and snarl of animals as well as the cry of people. He knew Kontra's men were out there and well able to take care of themselves. That meant his job was to keep those within their circle safe.

Sam barked a cry of alarm.

Turning, Acheron realized another would-be captor had leaped over the fire and into their circle. Elron and Caleb engaged him. While they probably wouldn't have trouble taking him, the downed human saw the opening for what it was.

The man slammed his fist into the distracted Sam's canine snout. Unfortunately, the wolf shifter was actually damn submissive and could only posture for so long. Between the pain and confusion, he yelped and backed off.

Acheron leaped from the table, hissing. His move drew the man's attention, who cried out in dismay and scrambled to pull his gun. Landing on the ground a few inches from the man's leg, Acheron swiftly crawled toward him.

When the human kicked, he barely missed Acheron. Using a pincher to snag the lace of the flailing man's boot, Acheron swung onto his jeans-clad leg. He used his second claw to slice through the thick fabric, giving him access to sink his stinger into the man's leg, then did it a second time, just to be on the safe side.

Due to the wounds' locations, his poison took longer to take hold. After an exceptionally vicious kick, Acheron flew through the air. He hit the ground and tumbled through the grass. Finding his feet, he tried to get his bearings.

The sight that greet him was the most gorgeous one he'd ever seen. A big-eared, long-limbed feline leaped through the flames. He landed on the human and bared long, deadly-looking canines.

The human gaped, then convulsed, before his eyes rolled to the back of his head, and he lay still.

After sniffing at the man, the cat levered off of his torso. The feline turned and padded toward Acheron. The black spots on the orangish-red and cream base of fur reminded Acheron of a leopard, but the longer limbs and bigger ears betrayed the cat's true breed.

This is my mate, my Rusty, a serval cat.

Another thought struck.

Just what the fuck is he doing here?

In the next instant, the cat lowered his head and rubbed a furred cheek against his plated body. If Acheron could have smiled in animal form, he would have. Instead, he rubbed his closed pincher against Rusty's feline face, doing his best to pet him.

When Rusty licked a swipe over his backside and nearly caught his tongue on Acheron's stinger, he decided that was enough of that for now.

Acheron shifted, changing swiftly from scorpion to man. When he'd finished, he crouched before the cat, which sat beside him, tall and proud, a pleased expression on a feline face. Chuckling, Acheron threaded his finger through the fur on Rusty's cheeks and proceeded to pet and scratch his gorgeous mate.

"Come on, Rusty," Acheron urged after a few minutes of

that. "Shift for me. Tell me what the fuck you're doing here." Scowling, he reminded, "You were supposed to be going after Korvyn."

At that moment, the fire diminished.

Acheron blinked a few times, his eyes adjusting to the sudden lack of brightness. When he could once again focus, it was just in time to watch the last of Rusty's shift. His naked lover lifted his head and met his gaze, then grinned.

"Hi."

Chuckling, Acheron held open his arms. "Hi."

Rusty lunged forward, closing the distance between them. As his mate wrapped his arms around him, Acheron did the same. He clutched his lover close as he rubbed his palms up and down his back.

Threading his fingers through Rusty's hair, Acheron urged his mate to tip his head down. He captured his man's mouth, thrusting between his lips. Lapping at his lover's tongue, mapping his mouth, Acheron took a few minutes to relish his unique, masculine flavor.

When breathing became necessary, he broke the kiss. He used his hold on Rusty's head so they could rest their temples together. Panting softly, he tried to get his suddenly scrambled thoughts in order.

Rusty's touch and taste was just that amazing.

Finally, the sound of people talking and moving around them registered.

Acheron sucked in a deep breath before glancing around. Shifters and their mates milled around the area. He spotted Kontra standing beside the table, his huge hand on Tim's shoulder. His people were carrying or leading away the humans that had been trying to capture them.

Meeting Rusty's gaze, Acheron asked, "What happened to the plan? To Korvyn?"

Rusty grinned. "As we drove away from you all, I scented

my brother." His smile turned fierce. "I realized they were close, so we circled back around and took them out. Korvyn is already on his way to Kontra's. Adam is driving him." Waggling his brows, Rusty continued, "So, a few of us came through the woods to see if you guys needed any back-up."

"Damn." A surge of relief Acheron could hardly explain flooded him. "That's—" He grinned widely. "That's fantastic." Pulling Rusty close, he whispered into his ear, "I am so glad that not only are you well, but Korvyn is safe, too."

"Me, too," Rusty replied before nipping at Acheron's ear. He chuckled huskily as he added, "Better yet, Kontra's people have the leader of the slave ring in custody. They're teaming up with Deputy Marrakesh Anderson's soon-to-be ex-boss, and they're going to take Wayland's whole network down."

While Acheron appreciated that news, with Rusty in his arms and the assurance that Korvyn was safe, he could think of so many other things to discuss.

"That's wonderful." Acheron tugged lightly on Rusty's hair, getting him to meet his eyes. "Shall we go to Kontra's place to check in with Korvyn?"

To Acheron's pleasure, Rusty shook his head. "Nope. I already talked to him." His mate's eyes narrowed as he swept over Acheron's naked form. "We should go home. I want to go for a run, then enjoy the moonlight on your naked skin as you fuck me by the stream."

More than on board with that idea, Acheron pulled away and rose to his feet. He held out his hand, pleased when Rusty didn't hesitate to take it, allowing him to pull him to his feet. Rusty grinned down at him, his expression heated.

Saying something that had always seemed more like a dream than anything, Acheron urged, "Take me home, my mate."

Rusty growled and nodded. "Clothes, then home."

Laughing, Acheron agreed.

ABOUT THE AUTHOR

Charlie started writing fantasy when she was eight, and after stumbling onto her first erotic romance at age nineteen, she realized her true calling. She now focuses on writing gay erotic romance, normally of the paranormal variety, with heroes of all kinds. With the help and support of her husband, Charlie finally fulfilled one of her life-long goals... move to acreage with her horses. You can often find her curled up with her laptop and a cup of tea or glass of wine, creating her next adventure. Charlie enjoys exploring the mountains of her new Oregon home on horseback, 4-wheeler, or motorcycle.

She can be reached at ch.richards2010@yahoo.com

Or visit her at www.charlie-richards.com